D0033695

Silhouette®

**MERLINE
LOVELACE**

Danger in the Desert

**CODENAME:
DANGER**

Vacation over...?

ROMANTIC

SUSPENSE

*Heart-racing sensuality and the promise of a
sweeping romance set against the backdrop of suspense.*

EAN

ISBN-13:978-0-373-27710-0

SRSATMIFC0111

She leaped to her feet, determined to get the hell out of there, and realized she was naked.

She grabbed Deke's shirt on the run. Got one arm in a sleeve. Skidded to a stop.

He'd reappeared, blocking the exit. His bare chest heaved and his eyes were savage. The gun, she saw on an icy shaft of terror, was still gripped in his right hand. In his left he clutched a green-and-white-striped cloth.

"What do you want?" She backed away, clutching his shirt to her breasts. "Money? My credit cards? Take them!"

"Jaci, it's all right."

He lowered the gun. In direct contrast to her panic-laced cry, his voice was calm, deliberate.

"This isn't what it seems. I'm not who I seem."

"No kidding!"

"Listen, I'm an undercover operative. I work for a U.S. Government agency, one you've never heard of."

"What?"

"I'll explain later. Right now you'd better get dressed. I need to call Kahil before they decide to come back and try again."

"Before *who* comes back?"

★★★

Become a fan of Silhouette Romantic Suspense books on Facebook.

Dear Reader,

Visiting the pyramids topped my must-do list for decades.
So I was thrilled when I finally got to climb into a saddle
and view them from the back of a camel. The experience
is one I'll never forget! It made such an impression I
knew I had to work both the amazing setting and that
dromedary ride into a book.

Yet my imagination had to work double time to keep up
with the characters in this story. They seemed to take
on a life of their own—and fall as deeply under Egypt's
timeless spell as I did. I hope you enjoy reading their
story as much as I did writing it.

Merline Lovelace

MERLINE
LOVELACE

Danger in the Desert

ROMANTIC

SUSPENSE

If you purchased this book without a cover you should be aware that this book is stolen property. It was reported as "unsold and destroyed" to the publisher, and neither the author nor the publisher has received any payment for this "stripped book."

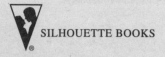 SILHOUETTE BOOKS

ISBN-13: 978-0-373-27710-0

DANGER IN THE DESERT

Copyright © 2011 by Merline Lovelace

Recycling programs for this product may not exist in your area.

All rights reserved. Except for use in any review, the reproduction or utilization of this work in whole or in part in any form by any All rights reserved. Except for use in any review, the reproduction or utilization of this work in whole or in part in any form by any electronic, mechanical or other means, now known or hereafter invented, including xerography, photocopying and recording, or in any information storage or retrieval system, is forbidden without the written permission of the editorial office, Silhouette Books, 233 Broadway, New York, NY 10279 U.S.A.

This is a work of fiction. Names, characters, places and incidents are either the product of the author's imagination or are used fictitiously, and any resemblance to actual persons, living or dead, business establishments, events or locales is entirely coincidental.

This edition published by arrangement with Harlequin Books S.A.

For questions and comments about the quality of this book please contact us at Customer_eCare@Harlequin.ca.

® and TM are trademarks of Harlequin Books S.A., used under license. Trademarks indicated with ® are registered in the United States Patent and Trademark Office, the Canadian Trade Marks Office and in other countries.

Visit Silhouette Books at www.eHarlequin.com

Printed in U.S.A.

MERLINE LOVELACE

As an Air Force officer, Merline Lovelace served at bases all over the world, including tours in Taiwan, Vietnam and at the Pentagon. When she hung up her uniform for the last time, she decided to combine her love of adventure with a flair for storytelling, basing many of her tales on her experiences in the service. Since then, she's produced more than eighty action-packed novels, many of which have made *USA TODAY* and Waldenbooks bestseller lists. Over eleven million copies of her works are in print in thirty countries.

When she's not glued to her keyboard pounding out a new book, Merline and her husband, Al, pack their suitcases and take off for new, exotic locations—all of which eventually appear in a book. Check her website at www.merlinelovelace.com for travelogues, pictures and information about upcoming releases.

To the Sensational Six. You know who you are. Thanks for making our jaunt to Egypt and the Holy Land an honest-to-goodness, once-in-a-lifetime experience.

Prologue

If she hadn't tripped over her own feet while gawking at the tombs in Cairo's City of the Dead, Jaci would never have spotted the tiny bit of green. It was almost buried in the dirt, tramped down by the centuries of mourners who'd brought their dead to be buried in the jam-packed maze of tombs that stretched for miles along the west bank of the Nile.

"Be careful, dear!" Susan Grimes, the seventy-something retired schoolteacher who sat next to Jaci on their tour bus, stretched out a quick hand to keep her from falling.

She didn't go down, thank goodness. She still

had a nasty bruise on her hip from the tumble she'd taken a week ago. Wishing to heck she was a little less klutzy, Jaci righted herself. That's when she spotted the bit of green. She thought at first it was a shard of glass or broken piece of plastic. Curious, she nudged it with the toe of her sneaker.

Mrs. Grimes leaned closer and squinted under the brim of her University of Florida visor.

"What is it?"

"I'm not sure." Jaci dug a little deeper with her toe. "Hey! It looks like a scarab."

It wasn't the first scarab she and her fellow tourists had spotted since arriving in Egypt early this morning. Cairo's souvenir shops were crammed with cheap plastic imitations of the beetle that ancient Egyptians associated with the creator god Aten.

This one, Jaci saw when she pried it out of the dirt, looked different from the fat little good luck charms hawked by souvenir sellers. Its body was longer, leaner. And it had lost one of its antennae. When she turned it over, the hieroglyphics on its belly were so worn they were barely distinguishable.

"Looks like a cheap fake," silver-haired Mrs. Grimes commented.

"Feels like it, too," Jaci confirmed. "Probably dropped by some other gawking tourist."

But a nice souvenir just the same. A keepsake of the trip she'd scrimped and saved so long for. *If* she could keep it.

She wasn't about to get crosswise of Egypt's stringent antiquities laws. Their tour group leader had cautioned them repeatedly about picking anything up at the pyramids or purchasing "stolen treasures" from supposed grave robbers.

And she *was* in the City of the Dead, with Saladin's massive fortress and the great mosque of Mohammed Ali looming above the jumble of tombs. The scarab Jaci had dug out of the dirt looked and felt like a modern-day, mass-produced version, but it wouldn't hurt to get the opinion of someone more knowledgeable about these things.

The tour leader had moved ahead, guiding her flock to the next intricately carved tomb, but the Uzi-toting guard who'd accompanied the group from the moment they'd boarded their bus was only a few paces behind.

"Hanif?"

"Yes, miss?"

"I found this buried in the dirt." Jaci uncurled her palm to reveal the little green beetle. "Do you think it's of any value?"

The curly haired Egyptian gave it a casual glance. Then he frowned and looked more closely.

"You found this?" he said slowly. "Here?"

"Yes."

When he took the scarab and turned it over, the crease between his dark brows deepened. The guard studied the markings for so long that Jaci was convinced she would have to forfeit her find.

"This is…"

He stopped, shook his head and dropped the beetle into her palm.

"This is nothing to worry you, miss. You may keep it."

"Are you sure? I don't want to get thrown in jail for pilfering an antiquity."

"No, no. Trust me, miss. You found it. It is yours. You must keep it with you."

"Well…"

"Jaci!"

Susan Grimes beckoned urgently from the entrance to a narrow alley lined with tilting monuments.

"Stay with the group, dear, or you'll get lost among all these tombs."

Chapter 1

A frigid November breeze rattled the branches of the chestnut trees lining a quiet street just off Massachusetts Avenue, in the heart of D.C.'s embassy district. It was late, well past midnight. The windows of the brick, Federal-style town house halfway down the street was shuttered and dark.

As far as most of the world knew, the elegant town house served as home to the offices of the president's special envoy. Only a handful of insiders were aware that the person appointed to the job of special envoy also served as director of OMEGA, an agency so secret that its operatives were activated only at the direction of the president.

One of those agents had just reported to the high-tech Control Center, which was tucked behind impenetrable walls on the third floor of the town house. An urgent phone call from OMEGA's director had yanked him out of the arms of the very accommodating flight attendant he'd bumped into at D.C.'s Reagan National Airport earlier that evening.

Deke Griffin, code name Ace, was no stranger to airports. Or flight attendants. A former air force fighter pilot, he'd ruptured a blood vessel in his eye when he'd had to eject during the first Gulf War. The injury meant he couldn't pull G's or fly high-performance jets any longer. But he could still fly the big heavies, which he did until he left the military to head his own aeronautical consulting service. Ace now jetted all over the world to advise developing countries on air safety.

The nomadic lifestyle suited him. As an added benefit, it provided a perfect cover for his covert OMEGA missions. He'd performed a good number of them over the years, but this one looked to be a real bitch. The political ramifications alone had Ace staring at his boss.

"Did I hear right?" he drawled in the West Texas twang that slipped into his voice at unguarded moments. "You're tellin' me we have an American tourist on the loose in Cairo."

"*Supposed* American tourist."

"…Who may be the focus of a small but fanatic religious sect determined to oust the current Egyptian president by any means possible?"

"You heard right."

Nick Jensen, code name Lightning, shoved a hand through his sun-streaked hair. Usually so urbane in Brioni suits and Italian silk ties, he'd pulled on well-worn jeans and a warm turtleneck for this hurried trip to the Control Center. Like Ace, he'd been yanked out of bed by a phone call, this one from the president himself.

Ace knew Lightning had been thinking about turning over the reins of OMEGA so he could devote more time to his wife and young twins. Everyone at the agency hoped that day wouldn't come soon. Lightning didn't look anywhere close to retirement tonight, however. His jaw tight, he'd focused his formidable energy on the American tourist at the center of what could be a diplomatic nightmare for the United States. A quick click of a mouse brought up her passport photo on the Control Center's wall-size screen.

"Her name's Jacqueline Marie Thornton," Lightning related tersely. "Goes by Jaci. Age, twenty-nine. Marital status, single. Residence, Gainesville, Florida. Occupation, assistant research librarian at the University of Florida."

Ace leaned forward, his gaze intent. The woman in the photo hardly looked like a radical subversive out to overthrow a government. Her soft brown hair just brushed her shoulders. Her green eyes stared straight at the camera. A tentative half smile curved her full lips.

But Ace knew all too well that appearances could be *very* deceptive. He'd been burned once by a sweet young thing who promised more than she'd ever intended to give. He'd ended up having to face down two very angry fathers—hers and his own. He'd only been eighteen at the time, but the lesson he'd learned from that fiasco had seriously impacted his outlook on relationships with the opposite sex.

As a result, Ace now confined his extracurricular activities to females who played the game by the same rules he did. No starry-eyed romantics for him. No nesters itching for hearth and home. Just savvy, fun-loving women looking for nothing more than a few hours of companionship. Ace couldn't help wonder what category Jacqueline Thornton fell into.

"She arrived in Cairo yesterday morning and joined a group of fellow travelers at the airport, all part of a tour organized by the University of Florida for alums and employees," Lightning continued. "Eight days and nights exploring the mysteries of Egypt's past."

"How many of those days will the group be in Cairo?"

"Four more, including today. That should be enough time for you to get close to her and find out what she's up to. I'm thinking it won't hurt for you to tap into the resources of your friend, Colonel El Hassan."

Ace nodded. He'd known from the moment his boss mentioned Egypt why he'd been tagged for this op. He and Kahil El Hassan had gone through undergraduate pilot training together at Vance Air Force Base in Oklahoma. With little else to do in their off-duty hours, the two bachelors had cut a wide swath through the adjacent town's available females. He and Kahil had stayed in touch over the years, each visiting the other whenever they happened to be in close proximity. Kahil was now a colonel in the Egyptian Air Force. He was also deputy director of his country's elite Military Intelligence Division.

"What have we got that indicates this Jacqueline Thornton is involved in a plot to overthrow the Egyptian president?" Ace wanted to know.

"Less than twelve hours after she arrived in Cairo, her name popped in cell phone chatter being monitored by Egypt's counterterrorist agency."

Lightning paused, and a dry note entered his narrative. "Seems this far-out religious sect I mentioned thinks she's a messenger sent by an ancient goddess."

"Come again?"

"Evidently there are a scarab and some hieroglyphics involved. Also a legend handed down through the centuries."

"You're kidding, right?"

"I wish. We pulled together a dossier. You can read it on the flight to Cairo. We've got you on a 6:20 a.m. departure out of Dulles."

"Roger that."

"In the meantime, we'll keep digging into Thornton's background," Lightning promised. "Rebel will act as your controller for this op. She's on her way in from Atlanta as we speak."

Ace gave a quick nod of approval. Victoria Talbot, code name Rebel, was relatively new to OMEGA but she, too, had once sported the silver wings of a United States Air Force pilot.

Word was she'd earned her call sign at the Air Force Academy, when she flatly refused to put up with some sadistic hazing that later got a whole bunch of academy officials, including the commanding general, fired. Her subsequent military training and the lethal tricks of the trade she'd picked up since joining OMEGA had quickly inducted her into the ranks of highly skilled operatives. Ace was more than pleased to have her working this op with him.

Along with his old friend. Thinking of the wild times he and El Hassan had shared, Ace extracted his cell phone from the case clipped to the waistband of his jeans.

"I'd better call Kahil and give him a heads-up."

The phone was no ordinary cell. It was sleek, super high tech and the brainchild of OMEGA's guru of all things electronic. Mackenzie Blair Jensen had cut back on her work for various government organizations since the birth of her twins. Except her work for OMEGA. Her ties to the agency went too deep, and the fact that she was married to its director kept her personally involved.

This particular Mackenzie-special was right out of a James Bond novel. It looked like an ordinary flip phone, but one touch of a key turned the user into a walking, talking biometric sourcebook. Sensors instantly verified the user's fingerprint and body heat signature. A built-in camera performed iris scans and facial recognition. A microchip-size voice synthesizer not only authenticated speech patterns but it analyzed them to determine if the speaker was under duress.

The phone also provided instant, encrypted satellite access for email, texting, GPS locator service, flight tracking, weather updates and more gee-whiz applications than a dozen iPhones cobbled together. Ace was still trying to figure out how to use half of them, but he knew enough to rouse his old buddy from sleep with one touch of a key.

"Kahil, you ugly bastard. I'm headed your way."

The long flight from D.C. to Cairo provided plenty of time for Ace to multitask.

His first order of business was a catnap to catch up on the sleep he'd forfeited to the sexy flight attendant. His second was to brush up on the Arabic he'd learned over the years from Kahil. Most of the phrases he'd picked up involved ordering beer or cursing at Cairo's kamikaze taxi drivers, but there were enough polite words sprinkled in there for him to order a meal and find his way around town. The rest of the flight he spent studying the dossier OMEGA had pulled together on this crazy legend. It made for some wild reading.

Supposedly, ancient tomb raiders had stolen a scarab from a small temple in the Valley of the Kings. The temple had been constructed by the legendary female pharaoh, Hatshepsut, and dedicated to Ma'at, the goddess of truth, justice, harmony, balance and cosmic order. For more than a thousand years, Ma'at's followers had waited for the scarab to reappear. The one who found it— they believed—would be a messenger sent from the goddess herself, heralding the need to restore order to a chaotic world.

Included in the dossier was a digitized photo of a statue now in the Cairo Museum. It depicted Ma'at in lapis lazuli and gold. She was seated on a throne holding an ankh in one hand. A headdress crowned by a towering ostrich feather circled her forehead.

The feather, the ancients believed, was used to weigh the heart of a dead person. If the scales balanced, it meant the deceased had followed Ma'at's forty-two principles for an orderly existence and his soul would pass into the afterlife. If not, the soul would be devoured by a demon, thus condemning the deceased to a final death.

Heavy stuff for a college librarian from Florida, Ace mused. He spent the last leg of the flight wondering just how the hell Jacqueline Marie Thornton had landed in the middle of a plot to restore Egypt to what some wild-eyed radicals believed was a natural cosmic order.

"Are you sure you want to do this, Jaci?"

Mrs. Grimes hovered a few feet away, facing the hoards of camel drivers who'd descended on their tour group the moment they'd exited their bus on the plateau overlooking the pyramids of Giza.

The late afternoon sun blazed down on the noisy, gesticulating group and made Jaci glad she'd left her lightweight jacket on the bus. She was perfectly dressed for a camel ride in sneakers, loose-fitting slacks and a short-sleeved white blouse with jaunty safari tabs decorating the shoulders and pockets.

One driver proved more vocal and persistent than the others. Shoving his way to the front of the crowd, he practically dragged Jaci to his shaggy mount.

"This way, madam. This way."

The ends of his green-striped headdress flapped as he steered her toward a beast with a high saddle and a tasseled bridle. The guard from their bus followed them and so did the stalwart Mrs. Grimes. The retired teacher glanced at the other tourists struggling to climb aboard their chosen mounts and reiterated her concerns.

"My guidebook says to be careful," she worried aloud. "Some of these camel drivers are real rip-off artists."

Jaci had read that, too, but seeing the pyramids of Giza from the saddle of a camel topped her must-do list. She wasn't about to forego the experience.

"Here, miss." Sensing he had his customer on

the hook, the doggedly persistent driver dragged off his headdress and plopped it on Jaci's forehead. "Now you are Bedouin."

Blinking, she adjusted the lopsided turban. The stained cloth reeked of sweat, human and otherwise. Resolutely, Jaci refused to even *think* about head lice. This was all part of the thrill of being in Egypt.

The three pyramids looming in the distance only heightened the exhilaration. This was what she'd scrimped and passed up pedicures for! This was what she'd dreamed about even before she'd joined her Thursday night Ancient Civilizations study group.

Eternal Egypt. Land of the pharaohs. Birthplace of a culture older than any other still in existence. Jaci could hardly believe she was finally here, seeing for herself the wonders she'd dreamed about for so long. She couldn't count the number of books she'd read, the hours of research she'd put into planning this trip.

No book or dry academic treatise could compare with the vibrant reality, however. The dust, the heat, the biting flies, the omnipresent and tenacious souvenir sellers…none of them could dampen her soaring spirits.

"Will you take my picture when I climb aboard?"

Still dubious but willing to oblige, Mrs. Grimes accepted the digital camera Jaci fished out of her canvas tote. The silver-haired teacher snapped several pictures while the driver boosted his rider into the saddle. Once Jaci had settled herself comfortably, she grinned and waved at the camera.

Then her camel pushed up on its hind legs.

"Yikes!"

She grabbed the pommel just in time to stop herself from catapulting forward, right over the animal's head. Her smelly headdress slipped down and covered one eye. She managed to stay in the saddle somehow but came close to tumbling off again when the creature got one front leg under him. Or her. Who could tell?

Swaying from side to side, the ungainly creature rocked up. And up. And up. Jaci looked down, gulping at the distance to the hard-packed dirt, and hung on for dear life. As if mocking her fears, the driver leaped aboard his own mount and brought it to its feet with seemingly liquid grace.

"We shall go to the edge of the plateau, yes?"

She unlocked one hand from the pommel just long enough to push the tail of her borrowed turban out of her eyes.

"Well…"

"You must see the pyramids by themselves. Away from the all these people. To do so is to see Egypt."

The guidebooks warned about this. Always, always establish a price up front.

"How much?"

"Very cheap, miss."

"How much?" she insisted.

The driver glanced at Hanif, as if calculating how much he could gouge from a member of the guard's group.

"Twenty dollars U.S."

"Done!" Jaci was too excited to haggle. She would have paid twice that for this experience. "Let's go."

The driver took her mount's reins and kicked his own into gear. The animals' shuffling, rocking gait took some getting used to. Side to side. Forward and back. Feeling like a rag doll strapped into the wooden saddle, Jaci hung on to the pommel with both hands while they descended the sloping plateau.

Then the magic of the pyramids engulfed her. There they were, right in front of her. The great tomb of Cheops, flanked by two lesser pyramids, burial chambers for the king's wives. They'd been constructed on a windswept stretch of desert many miles from the ancient capital of Memphis.

Egypt's present capital now formed a dramatic backdrop to these majestic structures. Cairo shimmered in a haze of heat and exhaust fumes just across the Nile, but Jaci had no eyes for the sprawling city. Her fascinated gaze remained locked on the pyramids.

As she and her guide got closer, she could make out the monstrous blocks of stone the builders had positioned one on top of the other. How, she couldn't imagine. The massive reality of these monuments seemed to make a mockery of every theory her study group had read or researched concerning the tombs' construction.

She was so enthralled by them that she didn't realize the camel driver had angled toward the dark green palms lining the river banks.

"Excuse me! Where are you going?"

"You must see the pyramids from the Nile. It is to see them as the ancients saw them."

"I'd like to, but…" She threw a glance over her shoulder. "I'd better get back to my group."

"It is not far. Just there."

Jaci injected a stern note into her voice. "Our tour is on a tight schedule. I need to get back. Turn around, please."

When the driver ignored her command and kept dragging on her camel's reins, the light dawned. How stupid was this! How stupid was she! In her excitement and eagerness to view the pyramids from the back of a camel, she'd fallen for one of the oldest tricks in the book.

Thoroughly disgusted with herself, she called out to him. "I get it now. Twenty dollars to approach the pyramids. How much to take me back?"

The driver kept going.

Okay, now she was pissed—and just a tad nervous.

"Hey! You! How much to go back?"

When he didn't respond, she bit down on her lower lip. This had ceased to be fun. Fighting to hang on to both her balance and her composure, she angled around and stabbed a finger repeatedly toward her group.

"Back! Take me back."

To her profound relief, she saw Hanif break away from the cluster of tourists and lope down the plateau in her direction. No, not Hanif. Another guard, this one in jeans and a lightweight sport coat.

He moved fast, thank goodness! Within minutes, he was close enough to shout something.

Startled, the driver twisted around in his saddle. When he spotted their pursuer, he muttered what sounded very much like a curse. Producing a short, braided whip from the folds of his robe he slashed the neck of his camel while yanking on the reins of Jaci's.

Her mount brayed and made an awkward lunge.

Jaci yelped and tumbled sideways.

Chapter 2

Talk about timing!

The moment Ace had cleared security at the Cairo airport, he'd contacted Kahil. As promised, his friend had obtained an updated itinerary from the local agency handling the tour for the University of Florida group. Ace had jumped in a rental car and arrived at the most touristy of all locales—the camel circus on the plateau above the Giza pyramids—just in time to spot his target lumbering off.

He'd hung back, mingling with the crowd while he observed this supposed messenger from Ma'at. It didn't take him long to decide the goddess had to be pretty hard up for emissaries. Jacqueline Marie Thornton looked just short of ridiculous with a greasy headdress tilted over one eye and an overstuffed canvas tote thumping against a hip while she bobbed along.

"Oh, dear."

That came from a smallish woman wearing a visor decorated with a University of Florida Gator. She was standing a few yards away, her worried gaze on the camels.

"I hope Jaci doesn't go too far," she said to another member of her group. "The tour leader warned us about these drivers."

With good reason. Ace had spent enough time in Egypt to know these guys had a real racket going here. They dressed like Bedouins, but most had never trekked across a desert. They also raked in so much from the hordes of tourists that many sported Rolexes and Air Nikes under their robes. Even the tourist police on their distinctive white camels rubbed their fingers together, demanding payment for every digital photo snapped by a gawking visitor. More money probably changed hands here at the pyramids than anywhere else in Egypt. And from the looks of it, his target was just about to be taken for double the usual fee.

She knew it, too. She'd contorted in the saddle and was pointing repeatedly toward the buses.

The incipient panic on her face elicited a twitter of dismay from her older traveling companion.

"Hanif!" The woman turned to an Egyptian in a cheap green suit ringed with sweat at the armpits. "Jaci wants to come back. Do something!"

The man—a guard assigned to the group, judging by the weapon bulging the back flap of his suit coat—cast a glance at the duo.

"Do not worry. They will return."

Ace hid a predatory smile. Perfect! He'd just been handed the ideal opportunity. His instructions were to get close to the target. What better way to win her trust than to rescue her from an unscrupulous camel driver?

He took off at an easy lope. Luckily, the sand on the plateau had been packed hard by centuries of tourists and plodding camels. Ace barely broke a sweat before he got within shouting distance.

"Stop, you son of a flea-bitten dog!"

It was one of the more useful Arabic phrases he'd learned from Kahil. Very handy when dealing with pickpockets and Cairo's suicidal taxi drivers.

The driver jerked around and cursed. Ace bit out an oath of his own when the man lashed his beast with a whip. The lead camel stretched his neck and broke into a hump-rolling gallop. When the second beast did the same, its rider shrieked and toppled sideways.

Christ! The woman was going to fall right out of the saddle!

Ace sprinted the last three yards and caught her just as she tumbled to the ground. He broke her fall, but she took him down with her. Grunting, they hit the sand and sprawled there, hips and legs tangled, while the driver and his camels galloped off.

"I...uh..."

Scrambling for purchase, the target dug an elbow into Ace's sternum. She levered up, then used her free hand to shove back the rankest turban he'd ever smelled.

"I'm so sorry. Are you okay?"

"I will be." Manfully, he repressed a grimace. "As soon as you remove your elbow."

"Huh? Oh!"

She squirmed, digging the bony joint in deeper. "Sorry."

Her face brick-red, she wiggled off him. She managed to mash her breasts into his chest in the process. The connoisseur in Ace didn't fail to note they were as lush and ripe as her lips even as the undercover operative took full advantage of her obvious embarrassment.

"No problem." He rolled to his feet and held out a hand. "Here. Let me help you up."

"Thanks. I...ouch!"

Her leg folding, she almost went down again.

Ace kept a grip on her hand and slid his other arm around her waist.

"Your ankle?"

"My knee. I banged it coming down." Biting her lip, she took a tentative step. "It's not bad. Just a little…"

When she broke off, wincing, Ace almost didn't believe his luck. He couldn't have scripted a better scenario.

"Better let me carry you back to your bus."

"No, really. I'm okay."

Ignoring her protest, he scooped her into his arms. The foul-smelling turban fell off, thank God. They left it in the dirt and started up the slope.

"I'm Jaci." Self-consciously, she hooked an arm around his neck. "Jaci Thornton."

"Deke Griffin."

"You're an American."

It was a statement, not a question, but he nodded anyway. "Yep."

"Are you on a tour, too?"

"Business." His civilian occupation provided the perfect cover. "I flew over to do some consulting. Just got in today and decided to stop by the pyramids on my way into town."

She gave him a sheepish smile. "I'm certainly glad you did."

Whoa! The woman's passport photo hadn't done

her justice. Ace could see himself in her eyes. The irises were greener than they'd appeared in the photo, almost as deep and verdant as the palms lining the Nile. Her shy smile and the light dusting of freckles across the bridge of her nose gave her a kind of girl-next-door appeal.

Definitely not his style. Aside from the fact she was his target and therefore off-limits, Ace went for less wholesome types. But he had to admit she made for a nice armful. Firm thighs, slender hips, narrow waist. The behind pressing against him wasn't bad, either. Not bad at all.

"Jaci!"

Led by the diminutive woman in the Gator visor, Thornton's travel companions rushed to greet her.

"We saw you fall! Are you hurt?"

"I'm okay. Just, uh, banged my knee a little."

"More than a little if you can't walk. You'd better have it x-rayed, dear. Hanif, where's the nearest hospital?"

The gun-toting guard frowned. "Not far. I will call someone to take her, yes? The rest of you can go on with the tour."

Jaci's heart sank. The next portion of their itinerary included a visit to the base of the Great Pyramid, time to explore the Sphinx and dinner at an open-air restaurant before the spectacular laser light show telling the history of these ancient monuments. She *couldn't* come all this way and miss the show.

"I don't need to go to a hospital. Really."

Hard to sound convincing while hefted in the arms of a total stranger. Embarrassed all over again, Jaci wiggled against his chest.

"You can put me down, Mr. Griffin. I'm fine."

Except she wasn't. When her tall, broad-shouldered rescuer eased her to her feet, she grimaced and had to lean heavily on his arm.

"I'll just…" She gulped, fighting tears of both pain and disappointment. "I'll just take a taxi back to the hotel and wrap my knee in ice. If it's still hurting tomorrow, I'll find a doctor."

"Oh, Jaci." Susan Grimes clucked her tongue in sympathy. "I know how much you were looking forward to the Sound and Light Show this evening."

"How about I offer a solution?"

The whole group, Jaci included, looked to her rescuer.

She'd had plenty of time to study his profile while he'd carted her up the slope. The strong, square chin. The gray eyes framed by lashes as black as his neatly trimmed hair. The faded, almost invisible scar above his left eyebrow.

She'd had time, too, to feel the muscles under

his lightweight tan sport coat. He'd carried her so easily, with such a sure, long-legged stride. No doubt about it. The man was buff.

"The show doesn't start until dusk," he said in a slow, easy voice that hinted at Southwestern roots. "That's a good three hours yet."

Three hours to sit in her hotel room with an ice pack on her knee. What a way to spend her evening! Jaci tried not to let her disappointment show while her rescuer continued.

"The wife of one of my business contacts here in Cairo is a physician. She operates a clinic just across the river. I could drive you there, have her check you out and bring you back to your group in time for the show."

"I couldn't ask you to do that! You have business to take care of."

A look she couldn't quite interpret flickered in his slate-gray eyes.

"My plans are nothing if not flexible. Hold on. Let me call my friend."

Like she could do anything else? Wobbling on one leg like a tipsy stork, she clung to his arm while he flipped up a cell phone. The fact that he had his business contact on speed dial told Jaci he dealt with the man on a regular basis.

"Kahil. It's Deke. Is Fahranna holding clinic today?"

His glance cut to Jaci. Smiling, he nodded.

"Good. How about giving her a heads-up to let her know I'm bringing in a patient?" He paused a moment, listening, and his smile took a wry tilt. "I'll explain later."

"I don't feel right about this," Jaci protested after he hung up. "You have other things to do besides chauffeur me around Cairo. If you'll give me the address of the clinic, I'll take a taxi."

"It's your call. But…" Her rescuer shrugged. "You might find yourself taking the *long* way into town. Cairo taxi drivers have elevated milking tourists to a fine art."

Jaci hesitated. During her day and a half in Egypt's capital, she'd found the people to be warm and friendly. Falling prey to a wily camel driver hadn't changed that opinion but it *had* made her a little more cautious.

Mrs. Grimes, too. Hands on hips, the silver-haired grandmother demanded some identification. "How do we know *you're* who you say you are and not some white slaver?"

"You don't," he replied with a nod of approval for her caution. "Here's my card. If it'll reassure you, we can give my operations center a call. I have someone on duty 24/7."

Jaci hovered on her good leg and peered at the card with Mrs. Grimes. The embossed lettering identified Deke Griffin as CEO of Griffin Aeronautical Consultants, based in Arlington, Texas.

"Aeronautical?" Mrs. Grimes read aloud. "Are you a pilot?"

"You bet," he replied, his mouth curving.

Later, much later, Jaci would kick herself for letting that cocky grin erase all doubts about driving off with a stranger. At that particular moment, though, all she saw were a pair of glinting gray eyes and an impossibly sexy smile.

"If you're sure it's no trouble?" she said a little breathlessly.

"No trouble at all."

"Then I'll take you up on your kind offer."

"Good. Keep the card," he told Mrs. Grimes as he scooped Jaci up in his arms again. "Have your tour guide call me in a half hour or so, and I'll let y'all know what the doc says."

The address on the card and that easy "y'all" confirmed Jaci's initial guess. The man sprang from Western stock.

Unlike her. Born and raised in Illinois, she'd followed her high school sweetheart's lead and applied to the University of Florida. Unfortunately, Bobby had used the year between his graduation and hers to dramatically expand his sexual horizons. Worse, he hadn't bothered to tell Jaci he wanted to continue his extracurricular activities until after she'd shown up for her first semester.

She'd endured a miserable four months while he strutted around campus with a variety of different women. Then his partying and late nights caused him to flunk out at the end of the semester. Jaci considered that sweet justice, but his abrupt departure from her life didn't lessen the sting.

She'd pressed on and completed her degree in library science. A subsequent job offer at the university's Architecture and Fine Arts Library had kept her in Florida after graduation. She'd never joined the lively on-campus party crowd, though—or the beach bunnies who headed for white sands and green waters every weekend. Her values were still solidly Midwestern, and her interests were more academic than social. Work filled her days, and an assortment of study groups took up several evenings a week.

It was one of those groups that had hooked her on ancient cultures—especially Egypt. Since joining the group, Jaci had dreamed of visiting this cradle of modern civilization. Three years of watching her pennies had made the trip a reality. She refused to let a fall from a camel ruin it!

She confided as much to her knight errant once he'd deposited her in the passenger seat of his rental car and had taken the wheel.

"I really, really appreciate you doing this. I can't afford to waste a minute of my time in Egypt."

He slanted her a quick look. "Have a full schedule laid out, do you?"

"Like you wouldn't believe! I've been planning this trip for ages."

She settled back in the seat, thinking of the months of study and preparation that had gone into her trip. Thank goodness for the Thursday-night group. One of the members had been born in Egypt. A former adjunct professor at the Health Science Center, Dr. Abdouh had retired from medicine years ago. He'd been a great help to Jaci in preparing for her great adventure.

She would have to email him about her near disastrous camel ride and send him a digital picture of the little scarab now tucked in her tote bag. Maybe he could interpret the markings on the beetle's back. He'd probably tell her the inscription read "Made in China," she thought ruefully. She didn't care. It was…

A shrill horn and the screech of tires cut into her musing. Gasping, she thrust out an arm to brace herself as a taxi shot into their lane. Her self-appointed chauffeur stood on the brakes and let loose with some Arabic. When Cairo's unbelievable snarl of exhaust-spitting traffic had sorted out a little, Jaci gave him a sideways glance.

"You must spend a lot of time in Egypt if you've learned to speak the language."

"I've picked up a few phrases. Not anything you'd want me to translate, though."

There it was again—that quicksilver grin. Jaci felt its impact all the way down to her toes. She curled them inside her sneakers and barely cringed when Deke had to swerve into another lane to avoid a donkey cart filled with cabbages piled to an impossible height.

Jaci twisted around for a better look. This was Cairo at its most vivid, she thought on a rush of pure delight. Donkeys were vying for road space with exhaust-spewing vehicles. Multistory concrete buildings were decorated with Arabic arches. Old men were fishing in canals dug by their ancestors millennia ago.

"So where's home for you, Jaci?"

The question brought her back around in her seat. "Gainesville, Florida. I'm an assistant research librarian at the university there."

"Guess that explains the gator on your friend's visor. The lady who took me for a white slaver."

"That's Mrs. Grimes," she said with an embarrassed laugh. "She's a former high school teacher. She takes nothing—and no one—at face value."

"Smart lady."

Very smart, Ace thought with a sideways glance at his target.

"Here we are."

He dodged a stream of oncoming vehicles and pulled through an arched entry into a palm-lined courtyard. Kahil's Egyptian-born, American-educated wife had opened her free clinic two years ago. Ace had been present at the ribbon-cutting ceremony. His company also contributed heavily to the clinic's operation. Dr. Fahranna El Hassan was nothing if not persuasive.

She was also tall, slender, gorgeous—and iron-willed enough to have tamed Wild Man Kahil. And now that she had her husband on a short leash, she'd moved Ace to the top of her list for reform—a fact she reminded him of after an attendant had showed him and Jaci Thornton into an exam room and the doctor burst into the room.

"Deke!" She threw her arms around him, digging her stethoscope into his chest as she kissed him on both cheeks. "Why didn't you give Kahil and me more warning of your visit? I have a cousin I want you to meet. She just might be the woman to wean you from your evil ways. Or…"

Her curious eyes swept over the female perched on the edge of an exam table.

"Have you brought one of your own for me to check out?"

"Curb your matchmaking instincts, Fahranna. I've brought you a patient."

All brisk business now, the physician addressed Jaci in her usual blunt manner. "I am Dr. El Hassan. And you are?"

"Jaci Thornton. Mr. Griffin, uh, Deke and I just met."

Fahranna lifted one delicately arched brow. "Did you?"

"We were at the pyramids. He was kind enough to bring me here after I fell off a camel."

"Ah, yes," she said with a wry smile. "The camels. What did you injure?"

"My knee, but it hardly hurts anymore."

"Let's take a look at it, shall we? You will have to remove your slacks. Deke, take yourself back to the waiting room."

To Jaci's relief, Dr. El Hassan's diagnosis confirmed her own. She hadn't broken any bones, just collected another bruise. The doctor recommended an ice pack if her knee started to swell and heavy-duty aspirin for pain.

When she walked Jaci to the waiting room, Deke tossed aside the newspaper he'd been perusing and offered his arm for support. Jaci took it with a shy smile that the physician didn't fail to note.

"You must come for dinner," she announced with a gleam in her dark eyes. "Kahil will want to meet the woman who moves his friend to such noble acts of chivalry."

Jaci opened her mouth to decline the offer, but her companion preempted her.

"You know I never turn down a free dinner, Fahranna. I'll give you a call later and set up a time that fits with your schedule and Jaci's."

Chapter 3

Ace waited until he had his target back in the rental car and was headed back to Giza to dig the hook in deeper.

"How long will you be in Cairo, Jaci?"

"Three more days."

"What does your agenda look like?"

"It's packed, morning to night. We're doing a breakfast cruise on the Nile, a visit to the pyramids of Saqqara and a whole afternoon at the Cairo Museum."

With its priceless gold and lapis lazuli statue of the goddess Ma'at, Ace remembered with a sudden tightening of his belly.

Coincidence? Could be. A trip to Cairo's famed museum was on every tourist's agenda.

"And," his passenger added with a flush of excitement, "we're going to the Valley of the Kings! We've got a whole day to explore Luxor and Karnak."

The Valley of the Kings, where Hatshepsut had constructed the temple to Ma'at. The same temple supposedly raided by tomb robbers more than a thousand years ago, giving birth to the legend that the goddess would someday send a messenger that it was time to restore cosmic order.

Another coincidence? Once again, it could be. But Ace had spent too many years in this business to take anything on supposition.

"What evening could you have dinner with Fahranna and her husband? You need to see their home," he added when she looked doubtful. "It's been in Fahranna's family for generations. The mosaic tiles in the entryway were supposedly fired in the same kiln as the tiles in the Grand Mosque."

"Really?"

She chewed on her lower lip, obviously torn. Ace reeled her in even further.

"The garden alone will make think you're in something right out of *Arabian Nights*. Moorish arches, marble fountains, swaying palms. Last time

I was there, they even had a nightingale warbling away."

"It sounds incredible."

"It is. How about tomorrow evening?"

She'd taken the bait. Her eyes were as bright as emeralds.

"If that works for you and your friends."

Ace knew damn well Kahil would make it work. His people were closely monitoring the sudden spurt of emails and cell phone chatter that mentioned Jacqueline Thornton by name. The colonel had already indicated to Ace that he wanted to make his own assessment of Thornton's motives for visiting his country.

"I'll give them a call later and let you know."

He cut the wheel to avoid a wobbly cyclist and decided to go straight for the jugular.

"So what brought you to Egypt?"

"My Thursday-night study group," she answered with a smile. "We meet once a week to explore ancient civilizations. We've been focusing on Egypt for the past year and…well, guess you could say I'm hooked."

"On?"

Her hand made circles in the air. "The culture, the history, the architecture, the rich pantheon of gods and goddesses. They all fascinate me."

"The gods and goddesses, huh?" He shot her a

quick look. "I don't know that much about Egypt's ancient deities, but from what my friends have told me, there were a bunch of 'em. Anyone in particular catch your interest?"

"Yes!"

Ace gripped the wheel as she angled toward him, her face alight. He paid no attention to her sparkling green eyes this time or the way the ends of her soft brown hair brushed her cheek. His entire being was focused on the seemingly artless disclosures that spilled from her lips.

"I'm thoroughly intrigued by the goddess Bast."

Bast? Was that another name for Ma'at? Ace knew most Egyptian gods and goddesses had changed names and shapes over the various dynasties. Had he missed that one?

"She was the Egyptian cat goddess," Jaci related eagerly. "Did you know the Egyptians highly revered house cats?"

"No, I didn't."

"It's true. Cats helped keep vermin out of grain supplies and would kill snakes, especially cobras. Owners would adorn their cats with jeweled collars, even let them eat from their plates at the table. If the owners were wealthy enough, they would have their household 'protector' mummified. Supposedly, more than three hundred thousand mummified cats were discovered when one of Bast's temples was excavated."

"Three *hundred* thousand?"

"I know. Sounds wild, doesn't it? Unless you're a cat lover."

"Like you?" Ace guessed.

"Like me," she agreed, grinning. "I've got two."

Figured. A college librarian with those wholesome, girl-next-door good looks. Not the type to go for a pit bull or a big, galumphing Lab.

"One—Mittens—is the laziest feline in the universe. She usually can't be bothered to do more than lift her head and twitch her tail when I come home from work. The other—Boots—is more lively. The little stinker has shredded two sets of living room drapes."

Good Lord! Mittens and Boots.

Restraining a grimace, Ace gave his passenger another quick glance. Was she for real? Or really, really good at projecting an air of wide-eyed innocence to disguise other, more suspicious activities? Damned if he could decide…yet.

He had pretty well made up his mind by the time he pulled into the parking lot for the Sound and Light Show.

Jaci Thornton had to be exactly what she seemed—the archetypal American tourist on the trip of a lifetime. When Ace had brought up Ma'at, she'd scrunched her forehead and said she'd read something about that goddess but couldn't recall specific details.

He'd then casually steered the conversation to Egypt's current political situation. Other than knowing the name of the current president and that he advocated reforms that had stirred opposition among some conservatives, Jaci didn't seem to have a clue as to who led the opposition.

She'd sounded so convincing, so sincere, that Ace was ninety-nine percent sure she was the naive, trusting tourist she appeared to be. Until he'd satisfied the remaining one percent doubt, however, he didn't intend to let the woman out of his sight.

He made sure of that by parking the car and insisting she let him walk her to the entry point for the Sound and Light Show.

"I'm fine, Deke. Honestly. My knee hardly hurts at all anymore. I can navigate on my own."

"Save your breath. No way I'm going to just dump you in the parking lot. Besides," he added as he hooked her arm through his, "I've never seen the laser light show. I'm thinking I might join you. If you don't mind?"

Mind?

Jaci's heart skipped a beat. Like she would *mind*

sitting under the stars with this kind, thoughtful, incredibly sexy man?

In the few short hours she'd known him, he'd rescued her from an unscrupulous camel driver, used his own body to break her fall and rearranged his schedule to get her to a doctor. He'd also promised to set up what sounded like a truly magical evening at his friends' home. Incurable romantic that she was, Jaci already viewed Deke Griffin as her own personal knight in shining armor.

"Of course I don't mind," she said in answer to his question. "But…"

She slowed to a stop and stood beside him in the parking lot. Chewing on her lower lip, she tried to find a delicate way to express her thoughts. There wasn't one.

"Look, I don't want to sound ungrateful for all you've done or, well, misconstrue your motives. It's just that I'm, uh, not…"

His eyes locked with hers. "You're not what, Jaci?"

Okay, she could do this. She owed it to him as much as herself to be completely honest.

She'd learned that painful lesson from her first and only love. If Bobby had been honest with her, if he'd told her about the "freedom" he'd discovered his freshman year in college, she wouldn't have followed him to Florida—or endured the agonizing humiliation of knowing he was out partying with a different girl every weekend.

Jaci hadn't dated all that much since college, but she made it a point to be totally honest with the men she *did* go out with. After all his kindness, she owed Deke Griffin the same courtesy. Pulling in a deep breath, she met his intent gaze.

"I'm not looking for a vacation fling."

Was that a glint of surprise that came into his eyes? Or approval? She was still trying to decide when his mouth curved and the glint turned positively wicked.

"Glad you let me know. Guess I'd better scrap my plans to carry you off to a remote desert oasis for a wild orgy."

Jaci had to laugh, but the erotic vision he'd painted sent a shaft of sudden and totally unexpected heat through her belly.

Now that, she decided, would be the adventure to end all adventures! Her vivid imagination concocted an image of the two of them alone in a silken tent, of her peeling off his sport coat and shirt. Popping the snap of his jeans. Gliding her palms over his taut belly.

She didn't realize her breath had shortened and her face had heated until Deke cupped her cheek with his palm. His skin felt smooth and cool against hers.

Good Lord! Was she really blushing like some Victorian schoolgirl? She didn't know—and when he dipped his head and covered her mouth with his, she didn't care.

The kiss reinforced her growing conviction she'd stumbled on an honest-to-goodness Lancelot. As his lips moved over hers, she could taste the heat in him, feel the strength in the arm he moved to her waist. Yet he lifted his head and ended the contact long before she was ready, darn it!

"I shouldn't have done that." His gray eyes were stormy now, his brow creased. "I'm sorry."

She let out a slow breath. "I'm not."

They stood in the dusty parking lot for several moments, his gaze on her face, hers on his. The honk of a taxi driver impatient to disgorge his passengers jerked them from their separate reveries.

"We'd better get inside," Deke said, a muscle working in the side of his jaw, "or we'll miss the show."

As they approached the modernistic building that formed the entrance to the laser show, Jaci leaned more heavily on his arm than she needed to. Her senses were still running riot from that kiss, and the play of hard muscle under his sleeve evoked another series of images—more X-rated this time. She pictured him naked this time, stretched out on a bed covered with jewel-toned silks and his body sleek with sweat as she straddled his hips and…

"…your ticket?"

She blinked. "Excuse me?"

"Do you have your ticket," Deke asked, "or do we need to buy another?"

"Oh! I've got it. Somewhere."

She fished around in her tote for several moments before finally producing the envelope of tickets included in the welcome packets provided by the tour agency. Deke paid for his and ushered her inside.

The entrepreneurs who'd come up with the idea of an ultramodern laser light show to tell the story of four-thousand-year-old pyramids hadn't missed a trick. The building giving access to the open-air amphitheater was crammed with cafés, bars, ice cream stands and, of course, the inevitable souvenir shops. One contained a window display of every object a tourist could desire. Her eyes widening, Jaci dragged Deke to a halt in front of a dazzling display of artifacts.

"Look, there's the Egyptian cat goddess."

She nodded to a slim, elegant feline with emerald eyes and a collar studded with colorful rhinestones.

"And there's a scarab just like mine!"

The muscles in Deke's forearm seemed to tighten under her hand. "You bought a scarab?"

Eagerly, she pointed to a dizzying display of beetles stacked one almost on top of the other. Most were round and fat. Only a handful had elongated bodies and one missing antennae.

"I didn't buy it. I found it in the City of the Dead."

She fished around in her tote again and produced a tissue-wrapped object. When she unfolded the tissue and held her prize up in her palm, Deke leaned forward for a closer look.

"It's only a cheap imitation," she said with a rueful smile. "Still, it's a fun souvenir."

She poked the chipped beetle with a finger and flipped it over onto its back.

"I'd love to know what these hieroglyphics stand for. One of the members in my Thursday-night study group is Egyptian. As soon as we get a break in our schedule, I'm going to snap a digital picture of the symbols and email it to him."

"Or," Deke said slowly, "you could let me send the scarab to Kahil. He'll know someone who can decipher the symbols. I bet he could have a translation ready when we join him and Fahranna for dinner tomorrow evening."

"I couldn't ask him to go to that trouble!"

"I can. The two of us go way back."

"I got that impression from Dr. El Hassan. But…"

Jaci fingered the green insect, oddly reluctant to relinquish it. Look at the good luck it had already brought her. Who would have dreamed she'd literally fall into the arms of a man like Deke Griffin?

"The symbols most likely say 'Made in China.'"

"Probably. Kahil will find out for you."

"If you're sure he won't mind…"

"I'm sure."

She dropped the beetle into his outstretched palm. She felt another odd pang when he pocketed the bug. The strange feeling disappeared when she reminded herself that she was now firmly committed to another evening with this fascinating man. The prospect made her heart beat a little faster as he ushered her out of the concession building into the viewing area.

With the last rays of the sun fading fast, the massive monoliths of the pyramids were now only faintly visible in the distance. The Sphinx, Jaci saw with a sudden catch in her breath, appeared much closer. In ancient times, the sandstone monument had marked the approach to the sacred tombs. Now it would form a dramatic backdrop for a display of ultra high-tech lasers.

That wasn't the only juxtaposition of ancient and

modern to strike Jaci. Like a Greek amphitheater, seating for the outdoor show descended to the desert floor in steep tiers. Instead of polished marble, however, these seats were stackable plastic lawn chairs.

Smiling at the incongruity, Jaci showed her ticket to an usher. Her tour ticket entitled her to a seat in the middle tier. Deke's, the usher informed them, was in the front tier.

"Not a problem," he assured her as they navigated the shallow steps. "Looks like there are plenty of empty seats. We can sit wherever you prefer."

Okay, she thought with a flutter just under her ribs. First his dashing race to her rescue. Then his self-imposed restraint during the kiss out there in the parking lot. Now his willingness to defer to her in matters as trivial as their seating.

How incredibly noble!

She could fall for this guy, Jaci thought. In a big way. That probably explained why she leaned on his arm again to go down the steps. And why she had to stifle a surge of disappointment when a familiar figure popped up and waved an arm in the air.

"Jaci! Mr. Griffin. Over here!"

Forcing a smile, she returned Susan Grimes's wave.

Just goes to show how quickly things can

change, she thought wryly. A few hours ago, she would have welcomed the older woman's company during the Sound and Light Show. Now, she had to battle a selfish desire to share the experience with Deke alone.

"What did the doctor say?" her friend asked when they'd joined her. "How's your knee?"

"No damage done. In fact, it hardly hurts at all anymore."

"That's wonderful!" Susan's glance shifted to Deke. The smile she gave him displayed no hint of her earlier suspicion.

"Thanks for taking care of our girl. She and I have only known each other for a few days, but we've become fast friends. I was worried about her."

"She's lucky to have found such a good travel companion," he murmured. "We all need to watch out for each other while visiting a foreign country."

There it was again. That crooked grin. It darned near melted Jaci into a puddle right where she stood. Mrs. Grimes, too!

"Oh, my," the silver-haired grandmother murmured faintly. "Here, why don't you sit next to me?"

"With pleasure. But I have to ask you to excuse me for a moment. I want to call my friends here in Cairo. Jaci's agreed to have dinner with them, and I need to see if they're available tomorrow evening."

Mrs. Grimes flapped a hand. "Go. Make your call. Jaci and I will sit here and drink in this incredible view of the Sphinx."

With a nod to the two women, Ace moved a few feet away. The crowd was buzzing with conversation, but he couldn't take the chance of being overheard.

His first call was to Kahil. The colonel answered on the second ring.

"Fahranna called me. She says she invited you and this Jacqueline Thornton woman to dinner."

"She did. I'll bring her to your place tomorrow night, if that works for you."

"It works."

The terse reply told Ace the internet chatter had increased exponentially. Kahil's next comment confirmed his guess.

"Tell me," his friend bit out. "Does Thornton have any idea of the controversy she's stirred?"

Ace sifted through his impressions of the woman he'd kissed mere moments ago. He still wasn't sure why the hell he'd given in to that insane impulse. Or why the taste of her lingered on his lips. Yet his answer came without hesitation.

"I don't think she has a clue."

"You know the stakes, my friend. Are you absolutely sure of this?"

"No," he was forced to admit. "Not yet. But I will be by the time I bring her to your home tomorrow."

Ace's glance zinged to the woman he'd seated beside her friend. He could think of a dozen ways to keep Jaci Thornton occupied until tomorrow night. To his consternation, most involved getting naked and extremely sweaty.

"You and I need to get together first thing in the morning," he told Kahil gruffly. "I want you to take a look at the scarab Thornton claims she found at the City of the Dead."

"She gave it to you?"

"She did."

"You move fast, my friend. But then, you always have where women are concerned."

"Look who's talking!"

"I no longer move at all," Kahil said sadly. "Fahranna has seen to that. But back to this scarab…"

"Jaci's curious about the markings on its belly. I told her you might be able to get them deciphered."

Kahil gave a bark of laughter. "I'm sure I can manage that."

"I thought so. See you early a.m."

Ace cut the connection and was about to slip the

cell phone back in its case when it vibrated in his hand. He glanced at the code on caller ID and felt his pulse gave a quick kick. The OMEGA Control Center didn't contact field agents unless absolutely necessary.

When he flipped up the lid, the ultra high-tech instrument did its thing. Less than two seconds later, Victoria Talbot, code name Rebel, appeared on the video screen.

"Hey, Ace." The honey-blonde tipped him a two-fingered salute. "Sorry I couldn't get to OMEGA HQ before you took off for Egypt."

"I'm just glad you're there now. What have you got for me?"

"It might be nothing. A mere coincidence."

"Tell me."

"I've been checking Jaci Thornton's connections at the University of Florida. Turns out she's a member of a study group that focuses on ancient civilizations. The group meets every Thursday night."

"She mentioned something about it."

"Did she also happen to mention that one of her study group members is Dr. Nasif Abdouh?"

"No. Who's he?"

"An Egyptian expatriate. He immigrated to the States twenty plus years ago. Time and distance haven't stopped him from keeping in touch with his old friends, though."

This didn't sound good. Ace's fist tightened on the phone as Rebel continued.

"I ran Abdouh's financials. Turns out the doctor has secretly funneled upward of eighty thousand dollars to friends in Egypt over the past few years. All, it appears, is to be used for the sole purpose of putting the opposition party in power."

Chapter 4

Well, hell!

Thoroughly disgusted with himself, Ace snapped the phone shut. Damned if he hadn't convinced himself Jaci Thornton was the innocent tourist she appeared to be. Their kiss a few minutes ago had pretty well wiped out his last lingering doubt, which only added to the chagrin now biting at him like Egypt's ever present sand gnats.

He'd kissed his share of women. Okay, more than his share. He was damned if he could figure out why the brief brush of his mouth over Jaci's had delivered such a punch to his gut. Or why the news that she had regular contact with a subversive totally pissed him off.

Had to be that light dusting of freckles on the bridge of her nose. That shy smile and wide-eyed delight. And that business about her pets. What kind of woman called her cats Boots and whatever the hell the other's name was?

The kind of woman Ace had made it a point to steer clear of. He wasn't home-and-hearth material. His missions for OMEGA were too dangerous, for one thing. For another, he'd yet to meet a woman who stirred more than a transitory rush.

This one, though...

Scowling, Ace looked across the amphitheater. Jaci sat next to Mrs. Grimes, both clearly visible thanks to the tall pole lights interspersed among the rows of seats. Engaged in an animated conversation, the younger woman leaned toward her travel companion. The glow turned her hair to a nimbus of soft-spun silk. The strap of her tote bag crossed diagonally between her breasts, outlining their shape.

Still frowning, Ace shoved his hand in the pocket of his sport coat and closed his fingers around the scarab. The beetle felt smooth in some spots, rough in others—as if it had been trampled by a busload of eager tourists. Or centuries of mourners bringing their dead to the tombs beside the Nile.

Ace found himself hoping the little bug was the fake Jaci seemed to think it was when the lights suddenly dimmed and floods lit up the Sphinx. The next moment a voice boomed through the now purple dusk.

"I am Cheops, pharaoh of all Egypt."

Even in the diminished light, Ace saw the rapture that illuminated Jaci's face. She looked like a kid peeking through the stair railing at the presents stacked under the Christmas tree.

Was she for real?

Ten minutes ago he would have said yes. Absolutely. Now he had to pump her concerning her connection to this character, Abdouh. Cursing under his breath, he forced a smile and joined the women.

The show was every bit as spectacular as Jaci had anticipated and then some!

Clever lighting projected the silhouette of a camel caravan marching across the desert. A huge image of the pharaoh, complete with blue-and-white striped headdress and a cobra crown, hovered in the now dark sky. Lasers in brilliant colors outlined the Sphinx and each of the pyramids in turn while Cheops related his story and that of eternal Egypt in a deep, resonant tone that rolled across the amphitheater. Jaci could have perched there in her plastic lawn chair and listened to him all night.

But the voice finally faded, the pyramids darkened and the crowd began to stir. Fighting a bone-deep reluctance to see this magical evening end, Jaci stuffed the camera she'd reclaimed from Mrs. Grimes in her tote and shifted to face the man beside her.

"That was absolutely incredible. I can't thank you enough for getting me back to my group in time to see it."

"My pleasure."

"So, uh, I guess I'll see you tomorrow evening."

"You will."

He offered his arm to help her navigate the stairs. Jaci took it even though the steps were shallow and her knee barely gave her a twinge. She liked the feel of his suede sport coat.

Ha! Who was she kidding? What she liked was the hard, muscled forearm covered by the buttery suede. Not to mention the world-class body attached to the arm. She leaned a little closer when they approached the tour buses lined up like racers in chock blocks, their engines spewing exhaust fumes into the night.

"Miss!" The guard assigned to their bus hurried forward. "You have been to the doctor?"

"Yes. Mr. Griffin drove me, as promised."

"And you are not hurt?"

"Just a little bruised."

"Good. That is good. Let me assist you onto the bus."

"Hang on a minute."

Deke held him off with an upraised palm and turned to Jaci. For a heart-stopping moment, she thought he was going to kiss her again. Excitement and anticipation danced across her skin.

"Are you totally whipped?" he asked.

"Not totally. Why?"

"I know you've put in a long day touring, but there's a club not far from here that has a patio overlooking the Nile. If you're not too tired, we could have a drink and watch the feluccas glide by."

"I'm not tired at all," she lied, "but you just landed in Egypt this afternoon. You're the one who must be completely exhausted."

One corner of his mouth kicked up. "Kahil will tell you I'm never too exhausted to have a drink with a beautiful woman."

Beautiful? Her?

Not hardly.

Jaci harbored few illusions about her looks. She had decent legs and okay breasts, but she came nowhere close to filling out a bikini like so many of the sun bunnies at the University of Florida. She considered her hair one of her best features. Thick and heavy, it gleamed like well-polished brass after a good brushing.

Which, she suspected, it sorely needed after a day in the sun and wind-whipped sand. What's more, she'd chewed off her lip gloss hours ago. In her sneakers, rumpled slacks and now wrinkled white blouse she felt about as far from beautiful as she could get.

Yet she didn't hesitate for a second. "A drink sounds wonderful."

"I do not advise this," the guard put in with a frown. "Cairo is very safe for tourists as long as they remain together. It is my responsibility to see Ms. Thornton and the rest of her group back to their hotel."

"I'll get her to the hotel," Deke told him.

"But…"

"I said I'll take care of it."

In the face of such confident authority, the guard had no choice but to relinquish his charge once again.

After the solemn majesty of the pyramids, the club Deke escorted Jaci into pulsed with vibrant, noisy energy. An exotic blend of Arabic and rock music throbbed through the speakers. Customers crammed the booths and tables, their lively conversations punctuated by laughter and the steady clink of glasses.

It was marginally quieter outside. A waiter showed them to a tiny table wedged between the wall and the iron railing ringing the patio. While the waiter went in search of an extra chair, Jaci grasped the railing and tried to absorb the incredible view.

She could see for miles both up and down the Nile. Struck once again by the juxtaposition of new and old, she let her gaze roam past modern hotels and apartment high-rises to floodlit mosques and minarets. And there, dominating all, was Saladin's mighty fortress.

The river itself held no less fascination. For thousands of years, the Nile had been the lifeblood of Egypt and the primary means of transportation within the kingdom. Judging by the watercraft plying the dark waters, it still was. Dinner and dance boats strung with bright lights cruised in both directions. Water taxis, ferries and motorboats buzzed past the slower craft…including one with a tall, angular sail.

"Omigosh!" Her heart thumping, Jaci clutched the iron railing. "You weren't kidding. You *can* see feluccas from here."

Deke crowded next to her for a look at the Arabic ship almost as old as Egypt herself.

"They cater mostly to tourist trade in this stretch

of the Nile," he commented, "but are still a main means of transport farther south."

"Our group is supposed to sail aboard one during our trip to the Valley of the Kings."

"Sounds like fun," he commented as the waiter reappeared with a chair and a request for their order. "What would you like to drink?"

"Orangeade, please."

"They're not supposed to but they can serve alcohol if you'd prefer something stronger."

"Orangeade is fine."

"Coffee for me," he told the waiter.

Silently Jaci applauded his choice. As she'd learned from her research, conservative Islam was making greater inroads into Egyptian society than it had in previous decades. The prohibition against alcohol was just one example. Another was the head scarves and black chadors many women now wore in public.

But not all of them. Educated women like Dr. El Hassan still opted for Western dress. So did the women at this popular nightspot. Jaci saw jeans and crops and even one miniskirt topped by gauzy blouses in a rainbow of colors.

When she brought her gaze back to Deke, he picked up the thread of conversation they'd begun earlier.

"You mentioned a Thursday-night study group

as one of the motivating factors that brought you to Egypt."

"I would have come sooner or later on my own, but the group certainly added to my determination."

"I can see how it would." Nonchalantly, he leaned back in his chair. "How did you get involved in it?"

"One of my coworkers at the university told me about it. Since I've always been interested in ancient civilizations, I was really eager to join. It was almost six months before they had an opening, though."

"Six months?" He hooked a brow. "Sounds like a tight group."

"It is. I was fortunate to get in at all. But my timing was perfect. They'd just wrapped up their study of the Hittites and were starting on Egypt."

She leaned her elbows on the rickety table and let her enthusiasm bubble over.

"We're so lucky to have a native-born Egyptian as a member of our group. Dr. Abdouh adds an incredible dimension to our discussions. He's a physician by training and has offered fascinating glimpses into ancient medical practices. Did you know the Egyptians did brain surgery to remove tumors more than five thousand years ago?"

"Wonder how many of their patients survived?" Deke drawled.

"More than you would imagine. Dr. Abdouh had us read translations of several inscriptions from the Tomb of the Physician at Saqqara. We think we're so smart, but you would be amazed at the skill of ancient physicians."

"I'm surprised the doctor didn't come along on your tour to act as guide."

"He wanted to, but I think there was some kind of problem with his visa."

"Leaving the States or getting back in?"

"I don't know. He didn't say and I didn't ask. Our group has strict rules about that. We gather to discuss ancient cultures, not personal issues." She met his eyes. "No politics or religion allowed, either. Not anything later than the second or third century AD anyway."

"Must be hard to shy away from current affairs," Deke mused. "Especially with a native-born Egyptian as part of the group. He's got to have a different take on, say, the current government here in Cairo than the rest of you."

"We've never discussed the current government."

He quirked a brow. "You're kidding."

"What can I say? We're more interested in pharaohs than presidents."

The arrival of the waiter interrupted their conversation. Deke picked it up again after Jaci had downed a long swallow of the tangy, refreshing orangeade.

"I hear what you're saying, but it still seems strange this friend of yours… What was his name?"

"Dr. Abdouh."

"Seems strange Abdouh wouldn't prep you a little more on modern Egypt for your visit."

"He follows the rules and keeps his personal views to himself." She made a face. "Wish my Saturday-afternoon Beethoven study group would do the same. Some weeks we spend more time talking grandkids and daughter-in-law problems than sonatas or concerti."

Deke cocked his head and gave her curious look. "How many of these groups do you belong to?"

"Four. Well, three. The fourth isn't really a study group. It's a more of a cat lovers coffee klatch," she explained with a laugh.

Jaci loved her life back in Florida. Her job was both challenging and satisfying. Her various study groups kept her intellectually stimulated. A large circle of friends provided companionship, and she had Mittens and Boots to cuddle up with during her rare free hours. Only now, hearing herself recite her litany of interests, did she realize how narrow and circumscribed they must sound to other people.

Like this intriguing, sophisticated man. He probably thought her a complete ditz for going on about kitty klatches and Hittites.

"What about you?" she asked. "I can only imagine what an adventurous life you must lead, jetting all around the world the way you do."

The Texan in him came out then. Stretching his long legs, he crossed his ankles. "Too dang adventurous at times, darlin'."

"Tell me," she demanded, propping her chin in her hands. "What exotic cities have you visited? How many other women have you had to rescue from camels or rickshaws or runaway trams?"

A belated thought occurred to her.

A very belated thought.

"And, uh, who have *you* got waiting at home? I'm guessing it's not two cats."

Shrugging, Deke answered the last question first. "You guessed right. Especially not two cats. One would be too many."

"You're kidding, right?"

"No, ma'am."

As Ace had intended, his comment roused his companion to an indignant defense of her precious pets. It also successfully deflected her probe into his personal life. That mission accomplished, he provided a counter to each of her passionate assertions concerning the superiority of felines over all other forms of animal life.

By the time their spirited exchange wound down, she'd finished her orangeade and her shoulders had started to droop. All Ace had to do now was get her back to her hotel and the room Kahil's men had bugged.

"You're tired. I shouldn't have kept you up so late."

"It has been a long day," she conceded with one of the shy smiles that evoked instant images of an apple-cheeked Doris Day. "But…"

"But?" Deke prompted.

Jaci hesitated, tapping a finger lightly on the table while she searched a way to express her appreciation without scaring the man off.

"I thought the pyramids or the Grand Mosque or the City of the Dead would top my list of all-time favorites in Cairo," she said slowly. "Sitting here with you…watching boats sail up the Nile as they have for countless centuries has made my Egyptian experience more personal."

So much more personal. Once back in Florida, she would fantasize about this man and this night.

And the one to come! She had dinner at his friends' home to look forward to. In a house right out of *Arabian Nights,* according to Deke. She hugged the delicious prospect to herself as they wrangled their way through Cairo's still frenetic streets.

The excitement that prospect stirred was nothing compared to the thrill that shot through her when Deke pulled up to the hotel entrance and insisted on escorting her to her room.

He didn't ask to come in for another nightcap, though. Probably because she was so exhausted she couldn't align her key card in the damned slot.

"Here, let me."

He slid it in, the green light blinked and the door clicked open. Instead of handing her back the key, however, he leaned an elbow on the doorjamb.

"Listen, Jaci…"

The intent look in his eyes made her stomach do a silly somersault.

"Yes?"

"I've got to take care of some business in the morning, but I have the entire afternoon free. I could clear my schedule for the following day, too. Why don't you let me…how did you phrase it? Personalize the rest of your stay in Cairo?"

As tired as she was, she had no difficulty formulating a dozen reasons to refuse the astoundingly generous offer. One, he shouldn't put his business interests on hold to squire her around. Two, she'd paid big bucks for this all-inclusive tour, and the money wasn't refundable. Three…

He cupped her cheek, and every rational thought flew out of her head. All she could think about, all she could focus on was the warmth of his skin against hers. Until he dipped his head and covered her mouth with his.

This kiss was different from the one they'd shared in the parking lot. Less tentative. More primal male, elemental female. The sensations that catapulted through Jaci were as timeless as the Nile.

Oh, man. She was way out of her league here. No one, including her high school sweetheart, had *ever* backed her against the wall. Or seduced her with just his mouth. Or demanded a response in kind.

She gave it. Willingly. Then she had to gasp for breath when he lifted his head.

Nostrils flaring, he rapped out a terse order. "You've got my card. Or Mrs. Grimes does. Call me at noon sharp. I'll pick you up, wherever you are."

Chapter 5

Ace arrived at the Ministry of Defense headquarters early the next morning. Kahil had a visitor's pass waiting and sent an underling to escort him through concentric rings of security.

"I am Major Nebbut, sir. Colonel El Hassan has told me many stories about you."

"Don't believe any of 'em."

Grinning, the major walked his charge through a series of perimeter checkpoints. At the headquarters' visitor's entrance, Ace removed his shoes to pass through a metal detector. Once inside, he was hand-searched. All too aware of the need for this vigilance, he let the security guard pat down his sport coat, shirt and jeans.

"This way, sir."

As at the Pentagon in Washington, D.C., these marble-tiled corridors echoed to the footsteps of military personnel in army khaki, navy whites and air force blue, with a healthy sprinkling of marines thrown in for balance.

Seeing all those uniforms gave Ace a distinct twinge. He'd thoroughly enjoyed his years in the military. The camaraderie, the urgency of the mission, the absolute certainty that someone was checking your six in combat and out. He'd never expected to experience that tight brotherhood of arms again until Lightning had recruited him for OMEGA.

"In here, sir. Colonel El Hassan is expecting you."

As deputy director of military intelligence, Kahil ranked a cramped suite of offices. The deputy's position was normally held by a general officer, but Kahil's combat record and demonstrated abilities had led to his appointment over other, more senior officers.

His heavy responsibilities hadn't erased the cockiness that was part and parcel of every F-16 pilot, however. The moment his secretary showed the visitor into his office, the colonel jumped up and rounded his desk.

"Ace, you son of a diseased camel." Still whipcord lean and tough, Kahil pounded his longtime friend on the back.

"Hello, Kahil. Ugly as ever I see."

It was an old joke—one that went back to their student pilot days at Vance Air Force Base. With his curly black hair and smoldering good looks, Kahil El Hassan had proved such a babe magnet that his entire squadron had lined up behind him for the leftovers. Hence his call sign, Nookie—as in lots of it. The nickname had stuck with him until he met Fahranna.

Grinning, the now-reformed Kahil waved Ace to a chair in front of his desk. "Have you plowed up any more potatoes, my friend?"

Another joke, this one a reminder of the time the nose gear on Ace's jet had failed on landing during a joint exercise involving eleven nations. His F-16 had corkscrewed wildly and skidded down the runway before finally coming to rest in an adjacent potato field.

"Not lately," he returned drily.

"Nor have you lost your touch with women, I see." Still grinning, Kahil dropped into the chair behind his desk. "I watched last night's surveillance tapes from the cameras in the hallway of Ms.

Thornton's hotel. They were very interesting, to say the least. I thought for a moment you intended to go above and beyond the call of duty."

"I thought so, too," Ace admitted ruefully.

He had absolutely no excuse for last night, other than the fact that Jaci Thornton had looked up at him with a smile trembling on her all-too-kissable lips. He'd gone into the kiss thinking it was the perfect way to convince her to jettison her tour and put herself in his hands. He'd come out wound tighter than a Chinese-made watch.

That reminded him of the business at hand. Reaching into the inside breast pocket of his sport coat, he produced a small, tissue-wrapped object. Kahil's face went still as Ace peeled back the tissue.

"This is what Jaci found buried in the sand at the City of the Dead. She thinks it's one of those mass-produced replicas you see in every souvenir shop."

"It may well be, my friend. It may well be. Then again, there is this flurry of email and cell phone traffic to consider. Someone obviously believes the scarab is very ancient."

Kahil took the beetle and studied it intently. As chief of security, he was a master at shielding both his emotions and his expression. But Ace had known him too long to miss subtle signs. The beetle excited him.

His dark eyes intent, Kahil stroked the scarab with his forefinger. "I'm certainly no expert, but this feels like malachite to me. And when this dull metal is burnished," he murmured as he traced the slender antenna, "I very much suspect it might shimmer like gold."

"Well, hell! You think the thing is for real?"

Carefully, Kahil turned the scarab over and traced the markings on its belly. He studied them for long moments before shaking his head.

"I don't know, my friend. As I said, I'm no expert. But I notified the director of the Cairo Museum after your call last night. He's got a team standing by to examine the scarab. I'll have it delivered to him immediately."

Kahil rewrapped the beetle and sealed it in a pre-addressed envelope. "Nebbut!"

The major hastened in from the outer office. "Yes, sir?"

"I want you to deliver this personally to the director of the Cairo Museum."

"Yes, sir!"

When the major saluted and performed an about-face, Ace felt the tendons in his neck cording. Dammit all to hell! He'd seesawed back and forth so much during this op that he was starting to get whiplash.

Those hours with his target yesterday afternoon and evening had all but convinced him she was the wide-eyed tourist she appeared to be. Then Rebel had dropped that bombshell about her study group pal.

Ace was sure he'd pumped Jaci dry about this Dr. Abdouh at the club last night. By the time he'd taken her up to her hotel room, he once again believed deep in his gut she was an innocent player in this dangerous game.

He'd relayed a report on that session to Rebel, then received one from her early this morning. After a long night of combing through contacts and databases, Reb confirmed she hadn't turned up any connection between Jaci and the Egyptian expatriate outside those Thursday-night sessions. No phone calls to or from his home or office. No personal emails. No tie in any way, shape or form to the funds Abdouh had funneled to his friends in Egypt.

Neither had Kahil, it turned out.

"We've traced some of these funds," he informed Ace grimly. "They were used to buy black market weapons. Glocks, Walther 9mm's, brand-new Kalashnikovs still in their shipping crate. Much of this is from Iraq," he added, "provided by your country to the Iraqi Defense Forces."

"Yeah, I know."

Ace raked a hand through his hair. The arsenal of weaponry provided to both Iraq and Afghanistan over the years kept coming back to bite U.S. troops in the ass.

"Who's buying them?" he asked Kahil.

"A ragtag fringe group of fundamentalists who want to take Egypt back to its pre-democracy days."

"The same group who've been waiting for Ma'at's messenger to appear?" Ace mused.

"It doesn't appear so, but I can't rule out a connection at this point. I'll have a better feel when I get a definitive report on the authenticity of the beetle."

"Speaking of which, I told Jaci you would return the scarab when I bring her to your place tonight," Ace said. "We need to have an acceptable substitute ready."

"I'll take care of it."

Nodding, Ace shoved out of his chair. Kahil rose as well but didn't let him off the hook that easily.

"So, my friend. About this Jaci Thornton. Like you, I'm very close to believing she is who you think she is. I shall know more tonight, after I assess her myself." He shot Ace a look. "But after watching those surveillance tapes, I must tell you she does not strike me as the kind of woman you would back against a wall."

"You think so?"

"I know so. Your women tend to back *you* against the wall."

"Okay, I admit I don't usually go for the innocent, girl-next-door type. You didn't, either, until a certain doe-eyed doc reeled you in."

A look of unholy glee leaped into his friend's eyes. "Are you saying this Jacqueline Thornton stirs more than mere lust in you?"

"Oh, for…" Exasperated, Ace headed for the door. "I only met the woman yesterday. Besides, she's my assignment. Lust is *all* I'll let myself feel for her, and you know damned well I won't act on it."

"That's true," Kahil acknowledged as he walked Ace through the halls. "I've never yet known you to seduce an innocent. If she *is* an innocent."

Ace was pretty sure he knew the answer to that. In the more figurative sense of the word, anyway.

The subtle inquiries Rebel had instigated confirmed Jaci dated occasionally. Odds were she wasn't a virgin. Not at twenty-nine! But she had no steady man in her life, and she certainly didn't come across as promiscuous in the profile OMEGA had built on her.

Nor, he could now confirm, did she send out the signals his personal radar was so attuned to. Those subtle signs he could pick up across a crowded bar or busy hotel lobby. The sideways glances. The slow smiles. The spark that told him a woman was not only interested but she played the game by the same rules he did.

Jaci was interested, all right. Her eager response last night provided ample evidence of that. It also told him she didn't play games. She hadn't held back, hadn't even pretended to hold back.

The contradictory feelings that were generated surprised the hell out of Ace. Any other time, any other woman, he would have backed off immediately. The fact that he didn't *want* to back off told him the sooner he wrapped up this op, the better.

Jaci knew she was in trouble the moment she spotted Deke descending the stairs at the Golden Salamander Restaurant.

The place was noisy and crowded with six busloads of hungry tourists. Laughter and boisterous conversation rifled through the long, arched hall. Monster iron chandeliers hung from the vaulted ceiling, adding to the ambiance of the waiters in traditional Egyptian robes and the round tables jammed around the dance floor.

Lunch, Jaci had explained to Ace during the phone call she'd debated about making all morning, included a belly dancing performance. She'd offered to skip it and wait for him outside the restaurant, but he'd told her not to miss the show. He would join her inside.

She was still debating the wisdom of that call when she spotted him. He wore jeans and a sport coat again, paired this time with a black turtleneck. With his short black hair, steel-gray eyes and confident stride, he turned more than one female head as he reached the bottom of the stairs and wove his way through the crowd.

When he smiled at her across the sea of diners, the last of the doubts she'd wrestled with all morning vanished on the spot. So she'd known the man for less than twenty-four hours? So that kiss last night told her she was playing with fire? She was on the trip of a lifetime, for pity's sake! Why not take a few scorch marks home as a souvenir?

"Hello, Jaci," he said in the lazy drawl that sent little shivers of delight racing down her spine. "How's your knee?"

"Not even a twinge today."

"Good."

She dragged her tote off the adjacent empty chair. "The show's just about to start. Mrs. Grimes and I saved you a seat."

"Thanks."

When he wedged in between the two women, the schoolteacher gave him a hard look.

"I understand you've invited Jaci to leave the group and take you on as her personal tour guide."

"That's right."

"I told her and I'll tell you that I don't think it's wise for a woman to go off on her own in a country where she doesn't even speak the language."

"She's not going off on her own," he replied calmly. "She'll be with me, and I know enough Arabic to keep us both out of trouble."

"Well, I've said my piece." The older woman paused, then gave him a grudging smile. "I'd probably do the same if I was forty years younger and didn't have a granddaughter close to Jaci's age."

"Forty years is no hill for a climber." His grin slipped out, quick and all male. "Dump this crowd and come with us."

Despite herself, Mrs. Grimes had to laugh. "Now wouldn't that be fun. The two of you hauling around an old lady."

"I'm serious."

"No, you're not," she retorted, still chuckling. "Just make sure you take care of Jaci, or you'll have an entire busload of Gators on your ass, young man!"

He was good, Jaci acknowledged silently. *Very* good. One quicksilver grin and he had Mrs. Grimes eating out of his hand. Two kisses, and she herself ached to go off with him to a desert oasis for that wild orgy he'd mentioned!

Lost in those delicious thoughts, the sudden crash of a gong almost made her jump out of her skin. The hollow beat of drums and tinkling cymbals followed. Eagerly, the crowd maneuvered their chairs around for a better view of the dance floor.

Jaci's pulse leaped in sync with the drums and cymbals. Dancing was as old as time, and Oriental dancing in particular embodied so many ancient traditions. Temples in Egypt and Persia contained carvings and inscriptions of dance moves as familiar today as they'd been three or four thousand years ago.

Carried away by what she'd learned about this art form in her study group, Jaci had joined a belly dancing class taught at the university's women's health center. There she'd discovered that the Hollywood stereotype of Middle Eastern dance was as far from reality as, well, a Hollywood stereotype.

Forget the spangles and transparent veils. Forget the seductress-out-to-tempt-a-man thing. From earliest times, Egyptian men and women had danced to express joy at weddings and harvests and festivals. At smaller family gatherings the sexes might dance together in lines or concentric circles. At public gatherings, they might dance in separate rooms or areas as dictated by religious or cultural beliefs.

Only in recent times had public belly dancing gained such popularity around the world. Although still frowned on by some ultraconservatives, the art form had produced such international stars as Dina and Fifi Abdo, currently rated the top performers in Cairo.

The dancer who swirled into the center of the Golden Salamander's hall, cymbals tinkling, was also pretty darn good! Her undulating hips and sinuous arm movements entranced Jaci so completely that she almost forgot the man whose shoulder was rubbing hers.

Almost!

A thunderous round of applause rattled the rafters at the end of the show. Smiling, the performer invited the women in the audience to join her on the dance floor for an impromptu lesson.

Mrs. Grimes, bless her heart, was game. "Come on, Jaci. Let's do it. Unless it will strain your knee," she added solicitously.

"My knee's fine, but…"

"Then let's do it," she insisted, pushing back

her chair. "I wasn't about to climb on one of those smelly camels, but I'll try this if you will."

Reluctantly, Jaci got up to follow her to the circle of women. She'd thoroughly enjoyed her belly dancing classes but had never danced in public. The idea of performing in front of Deke made her so self-conscious that she stumbled over the shallow edge of the stage. Flustered, she caught herself and took her place beside Mrs. Grimes.

The first moves were slow and easy, completed with much laughter from the group. All too aware of Deke's eyes on her, Jaci couldn't remember any of the hand gestures or hip swings she'd learned in class.

Gradually, she caught the rhythm. Lifting her arms, she began to sway along with their graceful performer. Thank God she'd opted for low-heeled sandals and a lightweight gauzy skirt this morning instead of jeans and sneakers. She would have liked to kick off the sandals, but even with them on she managed some credible moves.

Few people had any idea how strenuous belly dancing was. As the tempo increased, the hip swings became more pronounced, the abdominal rolls tighter and faster.

"Oh, my goodness!" Mrs. Grimes exclaimed after only a few moments. "I can't do this."

Huffing, she abandoned the dance floor. Other

women followed in twos and threes until only Jaci and the professional were left. The gleam of admiration in the other woman's eyes erased the last shreds of Jaci's self-consciousness. Head back, she gave herself up to the exotic music and the celebration of her femininity.

The dance ended with a crash of cymbals and a final, frenzied shimmy of hips and belly. After a second or two of awed silence, the crowd exploded. They surged to their feet, whistling, cheering and stamping their feet.

Flushed and laughing, Jaci responded to the wild applause with a gesture that gave all credit to the professional. As she turned to the woman, she spotted the guards from the various buses all congregated at the large round table where they'd eaten lunch. They were on their feet, too, clapping as enthusiastically as the rest of the crowd, although as Muslims they must have harbored mixed feelings about women dancing in public.

Then she made a half turn and caught Deke's gaze. The stunned expression in his eyes thrilled her all the way down to her toes.

Chapter 6

Ace couldn't believe it!

Every time he thought he had a handle on Jaci Thornton, she threw him another curve. This one damn near rocked him back on his heels.

Where was the clumsy tourist who'd tumbled off a camel? What happened to the girl next door whose life revolved around her studies and her cats? Who was this sensual, beguiling woman so confident in her femininity that she could express it in that incredible performance?

He wasn't the only one stunned by the transformation. Jaci's fellow travelers were still on their feet, cheering and whistling as she made her way back to the table.

"You were amazing!" Mrs. Grimes exclaimed. "Where did you learn to dance like that?"

"I took a belly dancing class last semester."

"Your moves were so fluid! So natural!"

"I know." She laughed and, reclaiming the seat Deke held out for her, said, "I'm usually such a klutz, but something in that music calls to me. It's as though…"

"As though what, dear?"

Her flush deepened. "It sounds really stupid, but the music takes me to another place. Another time."

"What time?"

"I'm not sure. All I know is that it's very distant from this one."

Ace froze. Literally. An icy coldness coated his veins as his mind formed the preposterous thought that she might actually be…

No! No way she could be channeling this ancient goddess, this Ma'at!

As if mocking his fierce denial, she made a hesitant admission. "It's weird, but the sensation has grown more intense here in Egypt. Ever since I found that scarab. Speaking of which…" Shifting, she turned to Ace. "Did you send my little beetle to your friend?"

Calling himself ten kinds of an idiot, he buried the ridiculous thought that had gripped him for a moment. He wasn't dealing with the supernatural here. Just one American tourist and some still-to-be answered questions.

"I delivered it personally," he assured her. "Kahil said he'd have a friend at the Cairo Museum look at it."

"Omigosh! The Cairo Museum. Now I'm really going to be embarrassed when they come back and say it's a machine-made imitation."

"At least you'll know for sure."

They all would, Ace thought grimly as he pushed back his chair.

"Are you ready to go?"

"I am." Eagerly, she grabbed her tote and rose. "Bye, everyone. I'll see you when I see you."

"Just be careful!"

Jaci acknowledged Mrs. Grimes's warning with a smile and a wave. She added another wave for the guard seated at the table across the hall. Hanif frowned and pushed back his chair, but Jaci was in no mood for another lecture about the need to remain with her group. This was her adventure, and she intended to squeeze every drop of excitement out of it. And that included spending as many hours as she possibly could in Deke Griffin's company.

She might as well admit it. This fascinating man pushed every one of her buttons. The faint leather-and-lime scent of his aftershave did a serious number on her concentration. Her skin sizzled when he put a hand to the small of her back to guide her up the stairs to the exit. And while they waited for the valet to bring around his car, all she had to do was glance up at his profile and the memory of his mouth covering hers in that hard, crushing kiss last night sent her pulse skittering all over the place.

"Where are we going?" she asked once they'd clicked the seat belts into place and he put the car in gear.

"Have you visited Saqqara yet?"

Jaci's excitement skyrocketed. The necropolis at Saqqara was the oldest in Egypt, predating the Giza complex by several centuries.

"No, I haven't. It's on our tour agenda for tomorrow."

"We'll alter the agenda. It's a nice drive through the countryside south of Cairo. If the traffic's not too crazy, we can get there and back in plenty of time for dinner at the El Hassan's."

She gave her ringing endorsement and settled back to enjoy both the ride and the company. By necessity, their conversation remained limited while Deke battled with city traffic. Once clear of Cairo, the high-rises gave way to the rural villages lining the banks of the Nile, and donkey carts appeared with increasing frequency.

As did more heavily veiled women. It was almost as though she and Deke had left the twenty-first century behind and traveled back in time. Black-robed women chatted while they scrubbed laundry in canals fed by the Nile or sat outside their homes to watch their children at play. White-robed men and boys worked the fields. Tall pigeon towers made of mud brick dotted the landscape, interspersed among lush green stands of palm trees heavy with ripe dates.

This was the real Egypt, Jaci thought with a sudden tightening in her belly. A rural society so attuned to the annual flooding of the Nile that it had endured conquest by Macedonians and Romans and a host of other invaders without losing its identity or uniqueness.

Then Deke turned onto the road leading to the Saqqara necropolis, and all trace of human habitation disappeared. The contrast was so startling that Jaci almost gasped. One moment, the road was shaded by tall, leafy palms watered for countless centuries by the Nile. The next, it emerged onto a barren stretch of sand and sky so vast there appeared to be no end to it.

And there, directly ahead of them, rose the Step Pyramid of Saqqara. Unlike the smooth-sided Giza pyramids, this one went up in layers like a wedding cake.

The entrance to the necropolis was equally

impressive. Excavated and reconstructed, the massive gateway led to a colonnade of marble pillars carved to look like tall palms. Jaci peered down the long corridor, wide-eyed with wonder, while Deke purchased tickets.

Fortunately, they'd arrived between waves of tour buses. Only two adventurous Germans with backpacks entered ahead of them. Unfortunately, that meant the souvenir sellers hawking everything from postcards to beaded Cleopatra collars had only limited targets for their wares. They darted among the marble palms, swarming Jaci, Deke and the Germans like human flies.

"Two dollar! Two dollar!"

Everything, apparently, cost the same. Jaci smiled and shook her head. Deke was more direct. A brief exchange in Arabic had the persistent entrepreneurs grinning and backing off.

"What did you say to them?"

"Nothing that bears repeating in polite company. Prepare yourself," he warned as they approached the end of the marble columns. "The first sight of the cobra wall always leaves tourists awestruck."

He was right, Jaci acknowledged as her stunned gaze took in the remnants of the intricately carved limestone wall that had once encompassed the entire necropolis. Hundreds of cobras looked down, their flared hoods a warning that all who entered were to respect the sanctity of this holy place.

The various temples dotting the sand and the windswept complex added to that sense of sanctitude. In them, legions of priests had performed the rituals necessary to ensure the kings entombed on-site enjoyed their life in the afterworld. There were a number of them, Jaci read from the brochure they'd been given at the entrance booth. Teti. Unas. And the greatest of them all was Djoser.

"He was the first king of the Third Dynasty," she read. "He came to the throne in approximately 2650 BC and immediately commissioned his vizier to begin work on his tomb. The architect built it of stone instead of the mud brick used in the tombs of his previous kings, thus ensuring it would endure for all time."

She gazed in awe at the stair-stepping structure at the far end of the plaza. It wasn't as tall or as massive as Cheops's monumental tomb, but the fact that it had survived far longer affected her in ways she didn't quite understand.

"We can go into several of the tombs," Deke commented. "If you're up for it."

As if she would miss them!

"Just lead the way."

Teti's tomb contained a giant basalt sarcophagus, star decorations on the walls and ceiling and

detailed inscriptions to ensure the king's resurrec-
tion. Mereruka's tomb featured a large hall with
a statue of the king and a sacrificial altar for the
various animals depicted on its walls. The tomb
that fascinated Jaci most, though, was that of the
king's physician. The wall reliefs portrayed an
astonishing array of the surgeries Dr. Abdouh had
told the Thursday-night group about. One series
showed physicians replacing a man's big toe with
a prosthesis. Another set depicted circumcision
rituals practiced in the Sixth Dynasty. The physical
attributes of the men lined up and waiting for the
surgeon's knife made Jaci do a double take.

Deke noted her reaction with a grin. "The artist
must have made them larger than life-size for il-
lustration purposes."

Either that or ancient Egyptians were excep-
tionally well endowed!

Next Jaci and Deke toured the site's museum
with its display of priceless artifacts missed by
centuries of tomb robbers. She spotted several
scarabs but none with her beetle's elongated body
and single antenna.

A growing need to reclaim her find gripped Jaci
as she and Deke drove back into the city.

They'd spent so many hours at Saqqara that there
wasn't time to detour to her hotel to clean up. But
they did manage a quick stop at a bazaar just inside

the city limits. Deke purchased chocolate covered dates, Jaci bought a bouquet of fragrant lilies for their hostess. Some moments later, they pulled up at a set of tall, iron gates.

Thankful all over again that she'd worn a tank top with cap sleeves that covered her shoulders and a skirt instead of jeans, Jaci hastily dragged a comb through her hair and dusted her shiny nose with powder. She was about to swipe on some lip gloss when Deke identified himself and the gates swung open.

Her jaw sagging, Jaci gazed at the palm-lined courtyard. Deke hadn't exaggerated. A huge, multi-tiered fountain splashed a joyous welcome. The Moorish arches surrounding the courtyard could have been transported from a caliph's palace. Ditto the glazed tiles that grabbed her by the throat when a maid opened the massive front door.

Mediterranean blues mixed with forest greens, brilliant reds and startling yellows to form a Tree of Life pattern that stretched the entire length of the entryway. Jaci almost hated to step on the exquisite tiles as the maid led her and Deke past a series of rooms furnished with a mix of traditional and modern.

The mouthwatering aromas of grilled lamb and fresh baked pita started her stomach rumbling. It was so loud that Deke shot her a quick grin just before they stepped onto a landscaped terrace. As he'd promised, the garden surrounding it was magical.

Somehow she managed to keep from gawking at the bushes dripping with perfumed flowers and the rectangular lily pond with another fantastic fountain in its center. Tiny white lights were strung everywhere and illuminated a tentlike gazebo constructed of billowing silks. Jaci barely had time to drink it all in before Dr. El Hassan and her husband came forward to greet their guests.

The physician had traded her stethoscope and lab coat for an exquisitely beaded and embroidered silk caftan in shimmering Nile green. Jaci swallowed her instant lust to own a loose-fitting tunic exactly like this one and returned the doctor's welcoming smile.

"You're not limping, I'm pleased to see. Did you experience any swelling of your knee?"

"None at all."

"Another patient lives to tell her tale," the dark-haired beauty pronounced, laughing. "Please, allow me to introduce my husband, Sheik Kahil Bakarim El Hassan."

Jaci turned to the tall, stunningly handsome man in pleated slacks and a white shirt tailored from a cotton so fine it might have been woven for one of the kings whose tombs she'd just explored.

"Sheik? I thought… That is, Deke said…"

Her host hooked a brow. "That I am the son of a leprous goat herder?"

"Actually, he told me you were in the air force."

"I am."

"A colonel, right?" she asked.

"Right, but you must call me Kahil."

She'd thought Deke Griffin was sex on the hoof! This dark-eyed, curly haired colonel/sheik gave him a real run for his money.

"And I'm Jaci."

"I'm very pleased to meet you, Jaci." He waved his guests to the table set under the billowing tent. "May I offer you a drink? We have tea and fresh lemonade. Or Egyptian beer, if you prefer, although I'm afraid it's somewhat strong for Western palates."

"Lemonade, please."

"Ace?"

Kahil caught Jaci's curious look. "That's the call sign we gave this rogue while we were both in undergraduate pilot training."

"Didn't Deke tell you how he earned it?" the colonel's wife asked with a gleam in her dark eyes.

"No."

"And neither will either of you," the subject of

their conversation interjected hastily. "I'd rather Jaci form her own opinions of my character."

"Too late. My opinion is already set in concrete."

Three pairs of eyes swung in her direction.

"Tell us," Fahranna demanded. "What opinions have you formed?"

Oh, Lord! Why in heaven's name hadn't she kept her mouth shut? She might as well climb to the top of the closest minaret and announce to the world that she'd developed a serious case of hero worship for one Deke Griffin.

"There aren't many men who would rescue a gullible tourist from a camel driver," she said with an embarrassed smile, "then take time away from his business interests to give her a personal tour of your city."

"Hmm." The svelte, slender doctor tapped a finger against her chin. "You're right. Not many men would give so generously of their time. Unless…"

Her voice trailed off, and Kahil moved smoothly to fill the small silence.

"I'll pour the drinks. Fahranna, my darling, why don't you tell the servants to bring food for our guests?"

The awkward moment passed, and Jaci breathed a sigh of relief. By the time Fahranna returned with servants bearing trays of appetizers, she was relaxed and enjoying both the surroundings and the company. She didn't need her hostess's urging to try at least one of the dozen different appetizers presented for her sampling.

The succulent olives swam in saffron oil, the goat cheese was ripe and aromatic. Sticky, sweet dates countered both those tastes, as did cold lamb kabobs and miniature pita pockets stuffed with chickpeas, onions and tahini.

Jaci was nibbling at a spicy fig roll when Kahil produced a tissue-wrapped object.

"Deke brought this to me earlier today." Carefully, the colonel unfolded several layers of tissue. "He said you found it in the City of the Dead."

"I did."

She itched to reclaim her beetle, but Kahil hefted it in his palm for his wife to see.

"It looks like malachite," she commented, leaning in for a closer examination.

"It is. I asked the director of the Cairo Museum to examine it." Kahil raised his eyes and met Jaci's. "He thinks the scarab is quite old. Eighteenth Dynasty, at least."

"You're kidding!"

Stunned, Jaci scrambled to sort through Egypt's dynastic history. If she remembered correctly, the Eighteenth Dynasty lasted from about 1500 to 1200 BC and included some of ancient Egypt's best-known rulers. King Tut. Hatshepsut, who'd proclaimed herself pharaoh. Amenhotep and his fabulously beautiful wife, Nefertiti.

The possibility that she'd stumbled across an artifact from one of the most glorious periods in Egypt's history sent Jaci's spirits soaring. Just wait until she told her Ancient Civilizations group about this!

The realization that she wouldn't be allowed to keep her little beetle brought her careening back to earth. Swallowing her disappointment, she tried to take the larger view. How many people could say they'd contributed to the riches of Egypt's past? At least she could enjoy the thrill of discovery and the excitement that came with knowing she'd added another footnote to a glorious history.

"How does your friend know the scarab is so old?" she asked eagerly. "He couldn't have had time to carbon-date it."

"He didn't need to. He used spectrography to confirm that the stone comes from a vein of malachite mined only in the Timma Valley."

"Where's that?"

"In what is now southern Israel. Legend has it that area is the location of King Solomon's fabled mines. But long before Solomon, Egypt ruled Timma."

Her heart pounding, Jaci glanced from Kahil to

his wife to Deke. Their expressions reflected her own growing surprise and astonishment.

This went beyond *anything* she'd imagined when she planned her trip. King Solomon's mines. Amenhotep and Nefertiti. King Tut. Their names and images whirled inside her head like a colorful kaleidoscope.

"Then, of course, there are these hieroglyphics."

Carefully, Kahil nudged the beetle onto its back. As she stared down at the markings, the oddest sensation gripped Jaci. Almost as though this was happening to someone else.

That wasn't surprising. Nothing, but *nothing,* in her neat, orderly, carefully scripted life had prepared her for this moment. Or, she thought as she shifted her glance again, for sharing it with someone like Deke Griffin!

His friend's startling revelations had Deke as tense and excited as they had her. His shoulders had gone taut, and the skin was stretched tight across his cheeks.

"What...?" Jaci swiped her tongue along suddenly dry lips. "What do the marking say?"

Silence descended—heavy, almost suffocating.

"They honor Ma'at, goddess of truth, justice and harmony. And," Kahil added slowly, "they tell of the one who will appear someday to true believers."

"Huh?"

"It is an ancient legend. One that goes back thousands of years."

His gaze held hers. Steady. Dark. Unreadable.

"Some say...some believe...the person who finds Ma'at's scarab is a messenger from the goddess herself."

Jaci couldn't help herself. She burst into noisy, unrestrained giggles.

Chapter 7

"I can't wait to tell my Thursday-night study group about this!" Jaci gasped between helpless giggles.

She, Jacqueline Marie Thornton of Gainesville, Florida, a messenger of the gods!

The preposterous notion set her off again. Clapping a hand to her mouth, she tried to choke back her bubbling laughter. The expressions on the faces of the others at the table kept it coming.

Fahranna appeared almost as entertained by the ridiculous notion as Jaci. Her husband's reaction was more reserved, although a sort of wry acknowledgment crept into his eyes as his guest continued to snicker behind her hand. He caught

Deke's glance, and the look the two men exchanged told Jaci they, too, saw the humor in the situation.

"Ah, well," Kahil murmured when Jaci finally swallowed her giggles, "it is only a legend. Egypt has as many such tales as the desert does grains of sand."

"I'll have to ask Dr. Abdouh if he knows that particular legend."

Kahil lifted a brow. "Dr. Abdouh?"

"He's one of the members of my Ancient Civilizations study group."

"The gentleman who was born in Egypt?" Deke queried.

"That's the one. As you can imagine," she said, turning back to Kahil, "he's been a wealth of information about ancient Egypt."

"I can see that he would be." Carefully, Kahil set the scarab on its nest of tissue. "You must tell us more about what you have learned from him."

Sternly reminding herself that she couldn't expect to keep such a precious artifact, Jaci dragged her gaze from the little beetle. She hesitated to display her limited knowledge in front of these sophisticated, highly educated Egyptians. But they were such gracious hosts they soon had her engaged in a lively dialogue that ranged from the

Nile's annual inundation to the system of collecting taxes in ancient times.

Their conversation continued over an incredible dinner of salad, rice pilaf and lamb grilled table-side on a charcoal brazier. They ate outside, with the fountain splashing and a panoply of stars over-head.

Talk segued to current affairs over coffee and dessert, and Jaci had less to contribute. It embarrassed her to admit her ignorance of modern Egypt. When she said so, however, Fahranna countered with the gracious observation that few visitors to the United States would be as knowl-edgeable of *its* history as Jaci was of Egypt's.

The conversation took a more personal turn after that. With a charming grimace, Kahil produced a thin, silver cigar case and turned to Deke.

"My sweet, adoring wife has rid me of all vices except these."

"Ha!"

"I'll bet!"

The simultaneous exclamations came from Fahranna and Deke. They grinned at each other across the table while Kahil assumed a wounded expression.

"She permits me one cigar after dinner, but I am flatly forbidden to light up anywhere in her vicinity. Will you walk with me, my friend, and join me in a smoke? You also, Jaci," he added politely. "We keep cigarettes for our guests, if you would prefer those."

"No, thanks. I never got into cigars or cigarettes."

"Very wise," Fahranna commented. Her gaze followed the two men as they strolled toward the far end of the rectangular pond. "It's taken me years to wean Kahil to one cigar a day. He's stubborn, that one."

"Sounds to me as though he's met his match," Jaci said with a smile.

"He has." Laughing, the dark-eyed beauty tossed her hair. "Most definitely."

They made a magnificent pair, Jaci thought with a little pang of envy. Both so accomplished and self-assured, with a big dose of gorgeous thrown in for good measure.

Just like their friend.

The pang took a sharp twist as her gaze centered on Deke. In the glow of the tiny white lights strung through the trees, he epitomized every secret female fantasy. Handsome and sexy and kind and considerate. No woman could ask for more—certainly not Jaci. Just looking at him made her chest go tight and a slow heat curl in her belly.

"The question now," Fahranna mused, breaking

into her thoughts, "is whether Ace has done the same."

"The same what?"

"Met his match."

"You mean…?" Jaci swallowed. Hard. "Me?"

"Why not you?" her hostess asked in obvious amusement. "You're intelligent, adventurous enough to travel to Egypt on your own and quite lovely. And, if I may say so, you're very different from the kind of women Ace usually consorts with."

Jaci tried to take that as a compliment. Unfortunately, her effort was blocked by a quick mental image of Deke's usual consorts. She had a sneaking suspicion they were sleek and cosmopolitan and not the least bit klutzy.

Then again…

Her glance zinged to the scarab nested on its bed of tissue. As if a cool breeze had suddenly drifted through the garden, the fine hairs on Jaci's arms lifted.

Was this all part of some cosmic plan? If she hadn't tripped over her own feet, she might not have spotted the beetle. And if she hadn't tumbled off the camel, she wouldn't have landed in Deke's arms.

Had they been fated to meet?

Had their destinies been entwined long before they met?

The possibility both thrilled and scared the dickens out of her. She'd loved before. With all her heart. She'd followed Bobby to the University of Florida, absolutely convinced they would spend the rest of their lives together. The shock of finding out he'd lied to her, that he hadn't had the decency or the courage to tell her he wanted out of their engagement, had shaken her belief in love itself.

That's why she'd thrown herself into her studies. Why she'd dated sporadically throughout her undergraduate and postgrad years. Why even today she filled her time with study groups and kitty klatches.

And why the mere thought that some divine predestination had landed her in Deke's arms made her wish desperately he'd stub out that damned cigar, drive her back to her hotel and finish what they'd started last night. Glaring at the scarab, Jaci formed a swift, silent prayer.

Come on, Ma'at. Do your thing!

A half second later her heart just about jumped out of her chest. Darned if the two men didn't flick their cigar butts into the shrubbery!

"So we're agreed?" Kahil eyed the two women sitting at the table at the far end of the lily pond. "This Jacqueline Thornton has no idea of, or involvement in, the controversy her extraordinary find has stirred?"

Ace gave a curt nod. "Agreed."

"You will notify your government. I will notify mine. Then, my friend, we must make sure she's on the first flight out of Cairo tomorrow morning."

"Agreed," Ace said again, suppressing a vicious stab of guilt.

He knew how much Jaci wanted to see Karnak and Luxor and the astounding collection of antiquities in Cairo's fabled museum. The realization that he would deprive her of those experiences put a kink in his gut. It didn't compare, though, to the knot that twisted his insides at the prospect of some anarchistic nuts using her as the central figure in a bloody uprising.

"I'll take her to the airport myself."

"Very well."

Like Deke, Kahil had long ago learned to disguise his thoughts. His smile when they rejoined the woman reflected only pleasure…and regret when Deke insisted he'd trespassed on their hospitality far too long.

"It's not yet midnight," Fahranna protested. "Cairo only now comes to life. Why don't we go to a club? Or to the Nile Hilton. Dina performs there. Jaci must see Egypt's most famous belly dancer."

If Ace needed any additional incentive to hustle

Jaci back to her hotel, that was it. His mind reeled off instant images of the sinuous, elemental performance he'd witnessed at the Golden Salamander.

"Jaci and some of her group tried their hand at belly dancing earlier today. She could give Dina lessons."

The rough edge to his voice sent Fahranna's brows soaring. She shot Jaci a look Ace couldn't quite interpret and raised no further objections to her guests' imminent departure.

"Before you go," Kahil said, "I wish to give you this."

He slid a hand into a pocket and withdrew another tissue-wrapped object. It was a replica of Jaci's scarab, polished to shining brilliance and threaded on a thin gold chain.

"It comes from the Cairo Museum," he informed her as he draped the chain over her head. "The director assures me it is of the finest quality. Not as valuable as yours, of course, but something you can treasure from your visit to Cairo."

"Thank you!"

Despite the city's perpetual traffic snarl, the drive to Jaci's hotel took less than twenty minutes. She spent those minutes fingering her scarab and thinking of the delightful evening she'd just spent. The night ahead offered even more possibilities.

Every nerve in her body tingled when Deke insisted on walking her through the lobby, into the elevator and down the corridor to her room. With each step, her breathless anticipation mounted. Torn between doubt that someone like Deke Griffin could be her destiny and the growing conviction he might be the one man in the universe for her, she slid the key card in the lock and propped the door open with one shoulder.

"Do you want to come in?"

Jaci's pulse went wild when his jaw tightened and unmistakable desire flamed in his eyes. Yet for reasons totally incomprehensible to her, he held back.

"I don't think that's a good idea."

"Why?"

"If you ask Fahranna," he said, reaching up to tuck a wayward strand of hair behind her ear, "she'll tell you I rarely refuse that kind of an invitation."

"As a matter of fact, she mentioned something along those lines."

"Damn! The woman knows too much about me and my past."

Jaci didn't care how well Dr. El Hassan knew him. Nor did she give a hoot about his past. Her only interest at the moment was the hunger he roused in her and the certainty that whatever happened tonight would decide her future.

If nothing else, she thought as a wild recklessness gripped her, she would always have the memory of Cairo.

"Why don't we just go with the flow?" she murmured, sliding her palms over his shoulders. "Or as Ma'at might say, yield to the cosmic order of things?"

She hooked her hands behind his neck, smiling at the surprise that flickered across his face. Then she went up on tiptoe and treated herself to the taste and the feel and the scent of him.

The heat flared as hot and as fast as it had last night. Sparks ignited low in Jaci's belly and spread like a California wildfire. She pressed against him, her mouth as eager as her body.

Deke's response was more deliberate. The tendons in his neck corded. His shoulders tensed. Ever so slowly, he slid his hands to the small of her back.

His restraint fired Jaci with something primitive, something elemental. The femininity she'd celebrated earlier in the day seemed to gather at her center, like a magnet drawing all parts of her toward a molten core. Her womb clenched. Her nipples tightened. Her breath came short and swift.

She pressed harder, her hips against his, her arms tight around his neck. And felt a spear of sheer exultation when his masculinity rose up to answer the urgent demand of her womanhood.

With an oath, he pushed inside and kicked the door shut. A quick fumble set the door chain. To Jaci's delight, his hands then got rougher, his mouth more insistent.

She responded in kind, attacking his shirt buttons and dragging the tails free of his slacks. Her hands planed the sculpted contours of his chest. He yanked her short-sleeved tank up and over her head. Her bra came off next, with a skill that left her half gasping, half laughing.

"You weren't kidding. You're good, Griffin."

Busy exploring her breasts, he flashed her a quick grin. "Thanks, darlin'."

Within moments her nipples were turgid and aching and her knees so weak they threatened to give out under her. Deke solved that problem by scooping her into his arms and carrying her across the room.

It was a standard tourist hotel room furnished in an Egyptian motif. Moorish arches topped the windows. The spread and drapes were printed with palms and colorful figures from antiquity. If Jaci leaned over the balcony railing, she could just catch a glimpse of the Nile through the maze of hotels crowding the river.

She didn't spare the decor or the view a single

glance as Deke deposited her on the bed. She lay there, aching for him, while he yanked the drapes shut. When he sat on the edge of the bed to remove his shoes and socks, she thought she heard the faint snick of Velcro.

She started to ask him about it but he stood up again to strip off his shirt, slacks and shorts. Jaci's mouth got drier with each article of clothing that hit the floor. And when he turned to face her, the erection jutting from its nest of dark hair almost made her swallow her tongue.

"Remember those wall paintings we saw this afternoon in the tomb of the king's physician?" she got out on a hoarse note. "The men with the, uh, exaggerated attributes."

Deke sent her a questioning look. "Yeah?"

"They have nothing on you."

Laughter leaped into his eyes. It was still there when he put a knee on the edge of the bed and leaned over her. "First time I've ever been compared to dead guys."

"First time I've ever had occasion to make the comparison," Jaci returned as she lifted her arms to welcome him.

He turned to stone, his body half covering hers. She looked up, startled by the frown that suddenly creased his forehead.

"Are you telling me you've never had sex?"

"What? No!"

"No, you haven't had sex or no, that's not what you're telling me?"

Of all the ridiculous conversations to be having with Deke's naked body hovering two inches above her quivering breasts!

"No, that's not what I'm telling you. But since we're on the subject, I'd better warn you my experience is probably somewhat more, uh, limited than yours."

His frown vanished, replaced by the grin that turned her bones to mush. "Not a problem. I'm willing to share my expertise."

More than willing.

Ace wanted this woman so bad he hurt. He'd held back last night, forced himself to remember his mission. He'd been sent to determine her involvement, if any, in the bizarre plot supposedly being hatched by a wild-eyed fringe group determined to bring down Egypt's present government.

As far as Ace was concerned, he'd completed his mission. Both he and Kahil had agreed. Jacqueline Thornton had no part in the plot swirling around her.

He was convinced of that…despite those odd moments. Like when Jaci was on the dance floor at the Golden Salamander. And a few minutes ago, when she made that crack about going with the cosmic flow. For a second there—just a second—he'd wondered again if she might actually have some spiritual link to this ancient Egyptian goddess.

When he looked down at her flushed face and quivering body, the crazy notion slammed into him again. If there was such a thing as cosmic order, this had to be it. She was all woman, timeless in what she offered. He was male and determined to take that gift.

Oh, hell! He was making this too damned complicated. He wanted her, she wanted him. Now his only need was to give her a healthy dose of hot, sweet pleasure.

He took his time about it. She was so open, so eager that her every gasp, every moan and shiver of delight wound him tighter and tighter. Rock hard and aching, he figured he'd better perform while he still could.

"Don't move," he ordered, planting a hard kiss on her mouth.

"Why? What are you doing?" she asked as he rolled off her.

"Making sure you don't take any incoming."

"Huh?"

"Once a fighter pilot, always a fighter pilot, sweetheart." Scooping up his slacks, Ace fished a condom out of his wallet and held it up. "We're always prepared to engage."

While she dissolved into giggles, he ripped the packet open and sheathed himself. The moment he rejoined her in bed, her levity vanished.

Ace braced himself on his forearms and felt an unaccustomed twinge of guilt push through the heat. He should tell her who he was—why he'd appeared on the plateau above the Giza pyramids when he had.

He'd get clearance from Lightning, he decided. Later. At that moment, all he wanted was to bury himself in her warm, welcoming flesh.

Two hours and two mutually explosive orgasms later, Jaci dropped into exhausted slumber. Ace cut off the lights and cradled her against him, waiting until her breathing evened and her body grew slack.

Strange. At this point he was usually calculating how to make a graceful exit from the hotel room. Now he had to fight the urge to hold her like this until they were both ready for round three.

Reluctantly, he rolled her onto her side and eased off the bed. Force of habit had him reaching for the ankle holster he'd hidden out of sight, under the mattress. One pat verified the weapon was still there and easily accessible.

Retrieving his cell phone, Ace dragged on his

slacks. He padded barefoot through the darkened room to the balcony. The sliding glass doors closed behind him, and Cairo's noxious night smog seeped into his lungs as he flipped up the phone.

Rebel's face materialized on the screen mere seconds later. A spiderweb of red showed in the whites of her eyes and her usually sleek honey-blond hair looked as though she'd combed it with a rake. Ace knew she wouldn't turn the desk over to her backup unless she dropped, though. He wouldn't, either.

"Yo," she said with a smile that belied her obvious weariness. "What's happening?"

"Tell Lightning that Kahil had the scarab evaluated by experts at the Cairo Museum. Looks like it could be the real thing."

"You're kidding!"

"I wish."

"So there may be something to this crazy legend?"

"If there is, Thornton doesn't know anything about it. Or believe it, for that matter. She couldn't stop giggling when Kahil told her the story."

They didn't usually go after targets who giggled or targets who got Ace rethinking his whole modus operandi concerning women.

"Kahil and I agree she's an innocent bystander. I'm going to hustle her out of Cairo tomorrow."

"Want me to make the arrangements?"

"Yeah, thanks. In the meantime, I..."

He broke off, his entire body coiling as a thin sliver of light suddenly lanced through the dimness across the room. Jaw locked, Ace watched the door to the hall crack open another inch.

"Well, hell," he muttered to Rebel. "We've got visitors."

The chain lock went taut. Ace was already yanking on the handle to the sliding glass doors when a pair of bolt cutters severed the chain.

Chapter 8

Always afterward Jaci would shudder every time she remembered the terrifying sequence of events that night.

Something jerked her from sleep. A thud? The rattle of the sliding glass door? When the mattress seemed to heave on one side of the bed, she raised her head and blinked in confusion at the shadowy silhouette looming over her. All she saw, all she had time to see, was a slice of his midsection. Dark slacks. Bare chest. A white-knuckled fist gripping a pistol.

Then a hard hand clamped over her mouth and pinned her to the pillow. Still confused and disoriented, Jaci reacted without thinking. She bit down hard on the fleshy part of the hand, heard a swift hiss and scissor-kicked off the bed. Or tried to. Her legs caught in the tangled sheets, and her panic-driven momentum sent her careening into her attacker.

"Dammit, Jaci, get down!"

Deke? That was Deke holding a gun on her? The terrifying realization spurred her to frenzy. Kicking, flailing, fighting desperately to get free of the sheets, she grabbed his gun hand with both of hers and screeched at the top of her lungs.

"Help! Help!"

She heard the sound of running feet, or thought she did. Hanging on for dear life, she wrestled with the man she'd surrendered herself to so completely such a short time ago....

"For God's sake!"

With a vicious curse, he wrenched free and shoved her to the floor beside the bed. She landed with a thud, still caught in the sheets. Frantic, she kicked them off and scrambled up enough to see Deke charge across the room and race through the door.

Light spilled into the bedroom from the hallway. Panting, Jaci stared at that patch of corridor. Terror roared in her ears. Her mind spun with shock and confusion.

Was he gone? Had her screams scared him off? Or...or... Oh, God! Was that the door chain dangling in two pieces?

He'd cut it, she thought on a fresh spurt of panic. Or shattered it when he'd bolted out. She was on her knees, scrambling for the phone beside the bed, when the fact that the door had already been open when Deke charged across the room penetrated her blind panic. She was trying to make sense of that when another realization slammed into her. The room phone was dead. There was no buzz. No beep as she repeatedly stabbed the keys. Nothing!

She leaped to her feet, determined to get the hell out of there, and realized she was naked. She grabbed Deke's shirt on the run, got one arm in a sleeve and skidded to a stop.

He'd reappeared, blocking the exit. His bare chest heaved, and his eyes were savage. The gun, she saw on an icy shaft of terror, was still gripped in his right hand. In his left, he clutched a green-and-white-striped cloth.

"Wh...? What do you want?" She backed away, clutching his shirt to her breasts. "Money? My credit cards? Take them!"

"Jaci, it's all right."

He lowered the gun. In direct contrast to her panic-laced cry, his voice was calm, deliberate.

"This isn't what it seems. I'm not who I seem."

"No kidding!"

"Listen to me. I'm an undercover operative. I work for a U.S. government agency, one you've never heard of."

"What?"

"I'll explain later. Right now, you'd better get dressed. I need to call Kahil before they decide to come back and try again."

"Before *who* comes back?"

When he hefted the striped cloth, she caught a whiff of an obnoxious—and strangely familiar— odor.

"Your camel driver, for one. I didn't get a good look at the other two."

Gaping, Jaci struggled with the astounding possibility that a camel driver and two accomplices had tried to break in to her room.

"They'd hit the bottom of the fire escape and jumped in their car before I got halfway down the stairs," Deke informed her. "You put up quite a fight, woman."

"I tend to do that when I wake up to find a pistol two inches from my nose!"

"Sorry about that."

He didn't look sorry. Just the opposite, in fact. His expression got scary again as he shut the door behind him.

"Get dressed," he said again. "I'll call Kahil."

"The...the room phone's dead."

"Not surprised. They probably used a jammer to scramble the phone and jimmy the electronic door lock. The security cameras in the hall, too."

When he flipped open his phone, Jaci decided she had two choices. One, she could take his word for it that he was some kind of government agent. Two, she could yank open the door while he was dialing the number and run like hell.

Her glance went to the broken door chain again. Now that her panic had subsided, she could see the links had been cut. She'd gotten up close and personal enough with Deke—if that was really his name!—to feel confident the man hadn't been packing bolt cutters anywhere on his person.

Then again, she'd had no idea he'd carried a weapon, either. Gulping, Jaci gathered her scattered clothing and retreated to the bathroom.

When she emerged some moments later, her room swarmed with people. A fully clothed Deke introduced her to two serious-looking hotel security personnel and a uniformed police officer. Another guest wearing one of the hotel's terry cloth robes had also materialized. He was one of Jaci's fellow tour group members and had heard what he described as a commotion in the hall.

"I tried to call the front desk," he related to the police officer, "but the phone in my room didn't work. Then I peeked through the door and saw this man." He pointed to Deke. "He was running down the hall—with a gun in his hand."

"Did you see any other persons?" the police officer asked in heavily accented English.

"No, only him."

"Thank you, sir. You may…"

He was interrupted by a fierce demand. "What's going on?"

A grimly determined Mrs. Grimes pushed her way into the room, hefting a bedside lamp in both hands like a baseball bat. Her short, snowy hair lay flat against her temple on one side and sprouted in all directions on the other.

"Jaci! Are you all right?"

"I am now. Took me a while to push my heart out of my throat and back down into my chest, though."

"What happened?" The older woman's nose wrinkled. "And what's that awful smell?"

Deke nodded to the green-and-white cloth now draped over the back of the desk chair. "One of Jaci's late night-visitors left it behind. Look familiar?"

"No. Should it?"

"Jaci was wearing a head scarf made of this

material when you took pictures of her aboard that camel."

"You're right! But how..." Mrs. Grimes stopped, her eyes widening. "Dear God! White slavers. I had the right idea but the wrong villain."

Her face drained of all color. Aghast, she turned back to Jaci.

"That man...that camel driver. He led you away from our group deliberately. I bet you anything he was trying to kidnap you." She shuddered. "He must have come back tonight to finish the job. Thank heavens Deke was here to foil his plans. Again."

The reason for Deke's handy presence suddenly dawned on Mrs. Grimes. She darted a quick look at the unmade bed but refrained from comment. Just as well. She'd given her travel companion more than enough to think about.

Jaci's mind was whirling with the possibility her aborted camel ride might have been the prelude to a *kidnap* attempt! She was still trying to grasp the incredible possibility when Colonel El Hassan appeared on the scene. Mrs. Grimes and the other tour member had gone back to their rooms, reluctantly persuaded by the presence of the police and security personnel. And by Deke's grim assurance that he didn't intend to let Jaci out of his sight until they got the situation sorted out.

The situation, as he termed it, took on even grimmer overtones with Kahil El Hassan's arrival. He brought several men with him and barked out orders like the senior officer he was. Since the orders were in Egyptian, as was his lengthy conversation with the men who'd arrived first on the scene, Jaci began to feel more like an observer than a participant. She huddled on the edge of the bed and tried to remind herself that she could get mugged in Gainesville, Florida, as well as Cairo.

But kidnapped?

Sold to white slavers?

Maybe. Women disappeared off the streets all the time, at home and abroad. She'd just never imagined it could happen to her.

Nor had she ever imagined she would wake up to find Deke Griffin standing over her with a gun! That searing image unsettled her almost as much as the thwarted invasion of her room.

She chewed on her lower lip, studying Deke as he and Kahil conversed out in the hall. Now that her terror had subsided, the realization that she'd made wild, uninhibited love with someone who claimed to be a secret agent was just starting to sink in.

Her lip was almost raw when the two men reentered the bedroom. The remainder of the crowd dispersed. At the request of Colonel El Hassan, hotel security officials went to review their surveillance tapes. The uniformed police officer departed with the green-and-white scarf in an evidence bag.

Now she was left alone with Kahil El Hassan... and the man she pinned with a hard stare.

"Who are you?"

The quick look the two men exchanged confirmed her growing certainty that they knew a whole lot more about what was going on here than she did. It also generated a wave of volatile emotions. Disgust at her own naïveté and embarrassment at how easily she'd been duped topped the list. But it was hot, searing anger that brought her off the bed.

"Who are you, dammit?"

"Exactly who I said I was," Deke answered.

"Right," she sneered. "The CEO of an aviation consulting company who, by the way, just happens to be a secret agent."

"That pretty well sums it up."

The laconic reply stoked her fury.

Jaci rarely got angry. She could probably count on the fingers on one hand the number of times she'd lost her temper. And she'd never resorted to violence! At this moment, though, she seriously considered hurling something heavy at Deke Griffin's head. In fact...

Propelled by the sickening certainty that she'd made a complete and utter fool of herself, she followed Mrs. Grimes's example. Two strides took her to the nightstand beside the bed. One swift yank separated the lamp's cord from the plug. With the heavy lamp in hand, she faced two extremely astonished men.

"One of you better tell me what's going on," she spit out, "or Fahranna will have to set a few stitches."

Kahil raised both hands and backed toward the door. "You tell her, Ace."

"Where are you going?"

"Out in the hall. I must notify my superiors of tonight's incident." His dark eyes glinted. "And tell my wife she may have to open her surgery."

He left the door open a crack, and for a long, taut moment the remaining occupants faced each other. Jaci didn't fool herself into believing she could carry out her threat. She'd witnessed Deke in action. Yet she would be damned if she'd relinquish the lamp until she got some answers.

"Anytime you're ready, Griffin."

Nodding, he scrubbed a hand over the back of his neck. He'd pulled on his loafers and the shirt she'd temporarily appropriated, but the dark stubble on his cheeks and chin gave him a rakish—and dangerous—air. The ankle holster he'd strapped on before Kahil and the others arrived added to that image.

"Okay, here's the thing. A good number of folks here in Egypt believe the legend linked to the scarab you found."

Stunned, Jaci dropped her arm. She'd formulated all kinds of wild conjectures since the attempted break-in. The possibility it might involve the legend Kahil had related earlier this evening wasn't one of them!

"Only a few hours after you found the scarab," Deke related grimly, "Egypt's internal security watchdogs started picking up email and cell phone chatter. The communiqués all had an American tourist at their focus."

"Me?"

"You."

Reeling, she tried to make sense of the extraordinary situation.

"So…?" She swiped her tongue over dry lips. "So were the men who tried to break into my room tonight after me or their precious beetle?"

"They don't know you left the scarab in Kahil's possession, so it could have been either."

He paused a moment before thrusting the knife in deeper.

"The situation is more serious than you may realize, Jaci. The people who buy into this legend have decided you're Ma'at's messenger. They want to use you as a rallying point for an uprising that would overthrow the present government. You can understand why Egypt's president would contact ours to express his concern."

"This goes all the way up to the *president?*"

"Yeah, babe, it does."

Jaci sank down at the foot of the bed. The lamp hit the floor as she struggled to accept the mortifying, degrading truth.

"So this supersecret government agency you work for sent you to check me out?"

He nodded.

At least he didn't lie to her this time. She gave him that much as her silly, stupid image of a knight in shining armor disintegrated.

She wouldn't cry. She *wouldn't!* Ignoring the hot sting at the back of her eyes, she lifted her chin.

"What did you decide, Agent Griffin? Am I Ma'at's messenger?"

"Come on, Jaci. You and I both know you didn't have a clue about the political turmoil you generated."

Okay, now she was not only naive but ignorant. Feeling like the biggest idiot on two continents, she raised her chin another notch.

"Just out of curiosity, did you reach that conclusion before or after we had sex?"

He smothered an oath and turned the question back on her. "What do you think?"

"To borrow your words," she said acidly, "I don't have a clue."

With another oath, he started for her. She stopped him with a steely glare.

"Answer the question, Griffin."

"Dammit, woman, making love to you wasn't part of the plan. If you must know, taking you to bed tonight went against all my training and instincts."

Pure, unadulterated pain piled on top of the anger and humiliation sloshing around inside Jaci's chest.

"Just what—" she stopped, bit down hard on the inside of her lip "—just what every girl wants to hear," she managed after a moment. "Her lover had to force himself to provide stud service."

"Oh, hell!" His mouth twisted in disgust. "That's not what I meant."

"At this point, I don't give a crap what you meant." She struggled to hide her hurt and humiliation. "The sooner you're out of my sight and out my life, the better."

"Yeah, well, I'm afraid that can't happen until I escort you back to the States."

"Back to the States?"

"Kahil and I agree. It's best for everyone concerned if we put you on the next plane out of Cairo."

His placating tone had the exact opposite of its intended effect. Incensed all over again, Jaci surged to her feet. Being lied to was one thing. Letting this man—or anyone else!—cut short the trip she'd dreamed of for so long was something else again.

"Get this straight, Griffin. No one's putting me on a plane out of Cairo."

"Jaci…"

"Colonel El Hassan has the scarab in his possession. He can—" she waved a hand, desperate to avoid termination of her trip "—he can say I turned it over to him. Confirm I'm just a visiting tourist, with no ties to Egypt. That should debunk this idea that I'm a messenger from Ma'at."

"*Should,*" the colonel echoed as he reentered the room, "being the operative word. Unfortunately, the group we're dealing with is quite fanatic. They obviously believe you're Ma'at's chosen one, as evidenced by tonight's attempt to take you and, we must assume, the scarab. For your own safety, Jaci, you must leave. Or…"

His dark eyes locked with hers. A shiver raced

down her spine. Almost as if she actually possessed the powers ascribed to her by the fanatics Kahil had just described, she sensed what he would suggest.

Deke must have divined it, too. With a low growl, he put himself between her and the colonel. "You'd better not be thinking what I think you are, buddy."

"I am...if you are thinking that Jaci could help us neutralize these radicals."

A muscle jumped in the side of Deke's jaw. His eyes as cold and hard as granite, he confronted his friend.

"There's no telling what these clowns might do if they get desperate. You can't put Jaci on the front lines."

"Egypt's national security may be at stake. I will do whatever is necessary."

The temperature inside the room seemed to have dropped a good twenty degrees. Jaci felt the ice as Deke issued a low, lethal warning.

"You'll have to go through me first."

"If I must."

"Hey!" Spurred by a welter of confused emotions, she thrust between the two men. "Remember me?"

Hands on her hips, she dragged in a deep breath and looked from one to the other.

"*I* found the scarab. *I'll* decide what role—if any!—I'll continue to play in this bizarre drama."

Chapter 9

Rebel had just deposited her third cup of coffee on the Control Center's main console when a yellow signal light flashed. Surprised, she threw a quick glance at the digital display of world times.

It was a little past midnight, D.C. time, and 6:10 a.m. in Cairo. It had only been a few hours since Ace's last report detailing the attempted break-in at the target's hotel room.

Raking back the honey-colored hair that insisted on falling over her forehead, Rebel answered the signal. Ace's face filled her computer screen. He looked, she decided with a quick kick to her pulse, distinctly unhappy.

"What's up?" she asked quickly.

"Change of plans. Thornton's agreed to El Hassan's harebrained scheme."

Rebel gave a low whistle. "Does she really understand what she's getting herself into?"

"Hell, no!"

The biting response made her blink. In all the time she'd worked with Deke Griffin, she'd never known him to lose his cool.

'Course, she'd never known him to call in a report from a target's bedroom in the middle of the night, either. Ace lived up to his reputation—and then some!—off duty. On duty, he'd always maintained a strict separation between business and pleasure.

Until Jaci Thornton...

What made the situation so damn intriguing was the fact that Rebel had combed through every scrap of data she'd dug up on Thornton. Aside from the woman's association with this suspicious character, Dr. Abdouh, she appeared as pure as the driven snow. *Definitely* not the type Ace's radar usually locked onto!

Interesting that she'd had the guts to agree to Colonel El Hassan's daring plan, though. Despite herself, Rebel felt a sneaking admiration for the assistant research librarian from Gainesville.

"Lightning called in a little while ago," she advised Ace. "He's on his way in. I'll bring him up to speed on the situation as soon as he arrives."

"Thanks."

"Do you need backup? Just say the word and I'll jump a jet out of Andrews. Or..."

Her glance went to the wall-size world map dominating one wall of the Control Center. Green lights designated agents currently inactive. Red lights signified those in the field. Aside from Ace, there were only two others out on ops. One of those two was just wrapping up a particularly hairy op in Turkey.

"Or I can divert Blade." Her mouth curved in a sly smile. "He's ten minutes from boarding a plane in Ankara. Nothing I'd like better than to yank him off that one and put him on another."

Ace's grim expression eased for a second. He, along with everyone else in OMEGA, had witnessed the titanic clash between Rebel and Clint Black, code name Blade, during her first week on the job. It was all due to a misunderstanding, but Rebel had been forced to knock Blade flat on his ass to get his attention. Both professionals, the two agents had smoothed things over. On the surface, at least.

"Much as I would enjoy having you pull Blade's chain," Ace said with a wry smile, "I've got Thornton covered for now. If I need help, I'll let you know."

"Roger that."

Rebel had barely disconnected when the blue bulb indicating Lightning's executive assistant was at her desk illuminated. Less than two minutes later, Lightning's designator lit up. Quickly, Rebel called downstairs.

"Hey, Chelsea. You're in early."

"Not early enough," Lightning's assistant answered in her well-bred, Boston Brahmin accent. "I thought I'd catch up on a little work before the boss arrived, but I haven't even had time to brew a pot of coffee."

Like Rebel, Chelsea Jackson was relatively new to OMEGA. She'd replaced silver-haired Elizabeth Wells, much beloved by field agents and technicians alike. The females in the agency appreciated the new assistant's cool efficiency. The males seemed to take her inbred reserve as a challenge to their masculinity, but Chelsea had shed that reserve to congratulate Rebel on the way she'd handled Blade. The two women had been friends ever since.

"I need to talk to Lightning."

"I'll let him know you're on the way down."

Rebel took a second to drag a comb through her hair and slap on some lipstick. Feeling somewhat revived, she hit the titanium-shielded elevator that would whisk her down to the first floor. Before exiting, she checked the monitor set at eye level. It wasn't likely any outsider would have arrived at the Offices of the Special Envoy in the short moments since Chelsea had cleared her, but security consciousness ran deep in Rebel's psyche.

Chelsea was at her desk, looking as cool and collected as always. "I'll buzz you in."

She pressed a hidden switch with her knee. Rebel nodded her thanks and entered the mahogany-trimmed office that had served a succession of OMEGA's directors.

As always, tanned and tawny-haired Nick Jensen roused instant and very different reactions. Rebel was secretly in awe of his razor-sharp intellect and respected his flat refusal to ask an agent to do something he himself wouldn't…or couldn't. But damn, the man was hot!

"I just got another report from Ace," she informed him. "He said Thornton agreed to Colonel El Hassan's plan."

The news surprised Lightning as much as it had Rebel.

"That's interesting. Nothing in the target's profile suggests she has the temperament—or the guts—to let herself be staked out like a sacrificial goat."

"Sounds like that's exactly how the colonel plans to use her."

"Is Ace good with this?" Nick asked.

"No, but he's going along with it. For the time being. He'll provide an update once he and El Hassan work out the final details."

"When does he anticipate that will happen?"

"Within the next few hours," Rebel replied. "He and Thornton are on their way to El Hassan's military headquarters as we speak."

Jaci stared out the passenger window of the car. With the hazy light of dawn, reality had set in. It felt as gray and all-pervasive as the mist swirling off the Nile. She contemplated the chill of both while a tight-jawed Deke wove through streets already crowded with the morning rush.

"This is crazy," he ground out for the second or third time.

Not as crazy as letting herself fall for a con man, Jaci thought miserably.

Oh, he had the law on his side. The entire U.S. government, as a matter of fact. Yet he'd manipulated her with the consummate skill and utter ruthlessness of a professional grifter.

And she'd taken the bait. Gullible and naive and just plain dumb, she'd actually believed a man like Deke Griffin could be attracted to her. Now she *was* the bait, despite Mr. Secret Agent's very vocal objections.

Cursing, he dodged a taxi and continued the heated argument he'd begun with Kahil at the hotel. "You're in over your head here, Jaci. The guys who want to overthrow the government are fanatics. Certifiable whack jobs. You don't know—none of us know—how violent they could become in their attempts to bring about their so-called cosmic reordering."

She refused to look at him. Staring through the swirling mist, she said stonily, "All the more reason to help Egyptian authorities identify the cult members."

"Kahil and his associates have other options at their disposal. They don't need to use you to lure these guys out in the open."

Enough was enough! Burying her misery, Jaci swiveled to face him.

"Listen up, Griffin. You've ruined the vacation I looked forward to for more than a year. In the process, you've reinforced the fact that I'm a total loser when it comes to judging men. You will *not* talk me out of doing what I think is right."

His jaw working, he kept his eyes on the unpredictable traffic. "We'll discuss the loser bit later. At the moment, I'm more concerned about your safety than your irritation that I didn't tell you the whole truth about myself."

She didn't doubt that! The man made a career of lies and half-truths.

"Irritation doesn't begin to describe what I'm feeling at the moment," she snapped.

"All right. Okay. You're pissed. We'll talk about that later, too." He pinned her with a dark look before returning his eyes to the road. "For now, just answer me this. Do you really think you're doing 'right' by jumping into the middle of a foreign country's political agenda?"

"I didn't jump," she pointed out frigidly. "I was pushed."

"My point exactly."

Scowling, he cut around a slow-moving truck so top-heavy with produce it looked as though its wheels would collapse. Horns blared and drivers gestured, but Deke ignored the hubbub.

"You don't have to get in any deeper, Jaci. I can turn around now and head for the airport."

If she'd known the details of the plan Colonel El Hassan had devised, Jaci would have taken Deke up on his offer right then and there.

She came close to it when she and Deke walked into the colonel's office and he informed them that he had everything arranged. The terse announcement made Jaci's already jumpy nerves take another skip.

Swallowing a rush of sudden doubts, she took the chair the colonel held out for her. He'd shaved and changed into a fresh uniform since responding to Deke's middle-of-the-night call. Silver wings gleamed above his breast pocket. A variety of other hardware decorated his epaulets and collar.

By contrast, Deke sported a night's worth of stubble above the open neck of the shirt Jaci had clutched to her front with both fists. The once-crisp cotton was a wrinkled mess. His pleated trousers weren't in any better shape. Yet his steely eyes remained locked on the colonel's as El Hassan detailed his plan.

"Even with the forces at my disposal, I cannot adequately protect you in the city. Not without potential harm to innocent civilians. And not if I want to throw out a net wide enough to catch more than a few small fish."

That wasn't what Jaci wanted to hear from one of Egypt's top security officials! Her stomach churned with doubts as he continued.

"So my people will spread word among your friends on the tour—and to any who may be watching or listening—that you have decided to take a side trip to see something of Egypt outside Cairo and the ancient temples."

"Where am I going?"

"To Jawal Oasis, in the Western Desert."

The irony of it hit her immediately. She'd fantasized about being carried off to a desert oasis, with Deke doing the carrying. Instead, she'd travel under military escort. So much for her erotic imaginings!

"Jawal is a traditional watering hole for Bedouin caravans," the colonel told her. "Very small and very isolated, which makes it possible for us to track every living thing that approaches."

The picture of a tiny pool ringed by palm trees and endless sand dunes leaped into Jaci's head.

"I'm certainly no military expert," she said hesitantly, "but wouldn't someplace that small and remote be *more* difficult to defend against an attack?"

"Not with an entire squad of air commandos only a radio call away."

"That makes me feel a little better."

"It should." El Hassan showed his teeth in a quick, slashing grin. "I trained every one of them myself."

"When do we leave?"

"Within the hour. I've sent someone to pack your things and check you out of the hotel. I've also called Fahranna. She'll have our driver deliver some of the robes she wears when we visit Jawal.

You will need them for protection against the wind and the sand. Also—" his grin took a rueful turn "—it's better if you go robed. My father is somewhat traditional in his ways."

"Your father?"

"Sheik Yousef El Hassan. He and his father and his father's fathers before him have held Jawal for centuries."

"Ooookay."

Jaci barely had time to process everything she'd experienced in the past few days. Now, apparently, she would be the guest of a genuine sheik. All that remained was to say adios to a certain lying, conniving secret agent. Stiffly, she got to her feet and held out her hand.

"Well, I have to admit our brief association has been…interesting. Good luck stalking your next prey."

"Save the goodbye speech. I'm going to Jawal with you."

She dropped her hand and any pretense at civility.

"Why? You did what you were sent to do. You checked me out, decided I'm not some wild-eyed anarchist and, oh, by the way, had a little fun on the side. You're done here."

"Not quite."

"I hope you're not traipsing out to the desert

expecting a repeat of last night's performance." She hid her still stinging hurt behind an angled chin. "I try not to make a fool of myself more than once with the same man."

"Dammit, Jaci…"

He threw a glance at Kahil. The colonel had folded his arms across the front of his uniform and was following the conversation with unabashed interest.

"You mind, El Hassan?"

"Not at all." The Egyptian waved a hand. "Please, continue."

"I will, when Jaci and I get some privacy."

"May I remind you this is my office?"

"And may I remind *you* there are still a number of incidents that took place during our undergraduate pilot training days your wife knows nothing about."

"Nor," an amused voice called from the outer office, "does she wish to know."

Jaci almost didn't recognize Fahranna when she strode in. The white-coated physician in Western dress had disappeared. So had the gracious hostess in her silk caftan.

This woman wore soft cream-colored boots, a turquoise scarf draped over her head and neck and a loose-fitting cloak with tiny, tinkling bells embroidered on the cuffs and hem. She carried a second cloak draped over an arm and a bulging carryall in her hand.

Her unexpected appearance brought her husband to attention. "Fahranna! Why are you dressed for the desert?"

"I'm going to Jawal with you."

"Absolutely not. This is a military exercise."

"Really? And Jaci is what? A sergeant in the Egyptian Air Force? A captain?"

"She is an integral component of the operation. You are not."

"She is also a woman alone in a country whose customs are unfamiliar to her. Especially the customs practiced by your father." Fahranna lifted her chin. "I won't allow her to walk into the lion's den without another woman for support."

"There are women at Jawal!"

"None who speak English very well," she shot back. "Do you really wish to show Jaci the purification rituals if she has her menses while at the oasis?"

A line of red singed her husband's cheeks. "Let's hope that won't be necessary.

"Let's," Jaci agreed faintly. "Look, Fahranna, I appreciate your generous offer. I really do. But there could be trouble."

"All the more reason for me to accompany you," the dark-eyed physician said with a shrug. "Kahil will tell you I'm a far better shot than him *or* his father. My ancestors on my mother's side were Berber," she explained. "The same Barbary Coast corsairs who bedeviled centuries of Crusaders on their way to the Holy Land."

And battled U.S. Marines on the shores of Tripoli, Jaci recalled.

Good Lord! Had she stepped into a time warp? Egyptian pharaohs. Barbary pirates. Bedouin sheiks.

"According to family legend," Fahranna told her with more than a touch of pride, "my grandfather many times removed could send an arrow across fifty yards of storm- and wind-whipped ocean and put it through the eye slit of a Crusader's helmet. I inherited a measure of his skill."

"More than a measure," her husband conceded with obvious reluctance. "I wish my commandos could shoot as well."

"Then we all agree. I travel to Jawal with you. Let's go to the ladies' room," she suggested to a shell-shocked Jaci. "You can change your clothes while Deke and Kahil ready a Land Rover for our journey."

"Deke isn't coming with us."

"Yes," he countered swiftly, "I am. The matter's not open to discussion," he added when Jaci started to protest.

She shut her mouth with a snap and marched out of the colonel's office.

Fahranna waited until she'd shut the door to the cramped ladies' room to pounce. "What was that all about? Why do you not want Deke to accompany you?"

"Before I answer that, tell me something."

Feeling as though she'd gotten lost in an *Indiana Jones* movie, Jaci leaned against one of the sinks lining the wall.

"Do you know what Deke does?"

"In his consulting business, you mean?"

"No, that's not what I mean," Jaci retorted.

"Ah, you refer to the work he does for your government."

"So you do know!"

"Of course. Not that he has ever said a word to me about it. Or Kahil, either." Amusement lit her dark eyes. "Despite all evidence to the contrary, men persist in thinking women are such naive twits."

The starch went out of Jaci's spine. Sighing, she slumped against the sink. "Some of us are."

"Perhaps. But not you, my friend. Look how you've tied Deke in knots in just a few short days. I didn't think I would live to see it happen."

"It hasn't happened, Fahranna. I'm just…just an assignment to him."

"Do you think so? Then our time at Jawal should prove extremely interesting." She handed the carryall to Jaci. "Here, I brought you clothes more suited to the desert."

At the physician's urging, Jaci shed her jeans and tank, then pulled on an ankle-length gown of soft Egyptian cotton in a vivid rose-and-blue pattern. Exquisitely embroidered at the cuffs and hem, the gown tied around the waist with a silk cord to keep from dragging on the floor. Over that, Fahranna draped a dark blue robe with billowing sleeves, also embroidered at the neck and cuffs.

"You will find these garments very comfortable at Jawal. The loose sleeves let air circulate during the day, and the long folds give warmth at night. Let me show you how to adjust the head scarf."

Deftly, she arranged the square of shimmering red silk embellished with tiny crystal teardrops.

"The straight edge goes across the forehead. This end you tuck over your shoulder so the fabric drapes your throat. When the desert wind blows sand at you like a thousand stinging wasps, you draw the cloth up to protect your mouth and nose, like so."

Jaci turned and peered through the narrow slit left for her eyes at her image in the mirror. Who was that strange, exotic woman? Certainly no one she knew.

With her Western clothes folded away in the carryall, she followed Fahranna out of the ladies' room to the front exit. Outside, they found Deke and Kahil waiting beside a dusty Land Rover. The men, too, had dressed for the desert. Deke wore a black robe and a white head cloth. Kahil wore a loose white under-gown, a black robe and a white head cloth banded with two black ropes. Both men, Jaci saw when a gust of wind blew back the folds of their robe, sported leather holsters buckled low on their hip.

Wondering what in God's name she'd gotten herself into, she hiked up her skirts and climbed into the backseat of the Land Rover.

Chapter 10

Jaci's Thursday-night group had spent an entire evening discussing Alexander the Great's grueling march across the desert to consult the oracle at the Siwa Oasis.

From those detailed studies, she knew Siwa was one of five large oases that had served as a lifeline for caravans crossing the desert for thousands of years. She also knew there were many smaller watering holes. She'd just never expected to catch her first glimpse of one of these perfect green gems after jouncing along a pitted asphalt road, then abandoning the road for a beaten dirt track and, finally, churning through miles of shifting sand. By the time the Land Rover topped a rise and Jawal Oasis appeared in the distance, she was hot, tired and seriously questioning her sanity.

Especially after sharing the Land Rover's cramped backseat with Deke for most of the trip. The bumps and jolts had sent her shoulder into his, and their knees had connected so often that Jaci got a cramp trying to corral her leg. Then they'd had to stretch and work out the kinks. Of course she'd lost her balance trying to clamber over her tote and had practically fallen into his arms.

His grip when he caught her roused instant, searing memories of last night. Disgusted with herself all over again for being so gullible, Jaci spoke barely two words to Deke for the rest of the trip…until they topped a mountainous sand dune and spotted Jawal Oasis far below.

Surprised, she put her nose to the window. "It's sunk so low!"

"Most desert oases are," Deke answered, leaning his shoulder into hers for a better look. "Centuries of wind and erosion blow away the sand and cause depressions that go down deep enough to tap into the water table."

"The great Kharga Oasis south of here is more than a hundred miles long," Fahranna supplied from the front seat, "and sunk well below sea level."

Jawal didn't look anywhere close to a hundred miles long. At best, Jaci guessed, the oblong slash of verdant green stretched for a mile. Maybe two. She couldn't imagine how it had held out for so many centuries against the sand dunes that towered over it on all sides.

After Fahranna's comments about her father-in-law, Jaci had expected to see strings of camels and goat-hair tents pitched among the palms. The camels were there. Milk producers, pack animals and sleek racing camels worth tens of thousands of dollars, according to Kahil. But instead of tents, the oasis boasted what looked like a dozen or so mud-brick buildings, all seemingly stacked one on top of the other.

"Jawal has no electricity or phone service," the colonel warned as he put the Land Rover in gear, "so I wasn't able to advise my father of our arrival."

"But he'll send a party out to greet us," Fahranna added drily. "Nothing, not even a scorpion, moves in this part of the desert without Sheik Yousef's knowledge."

As if to underscore her comment, a dazzling light flashed for an instant atop a distant dune. When it flashed again, Jaci realized watchers were using mirrors to signal the oasis. Just a few minutes later, four men raced out of the palms. Their camels moved with an ungainly grace and speed that sent them flying across the sand.

The riders wore dark blue robes that flapped in the wind and the traditional white head cloth banded by corded ropes. Only after they got closer did Jaci note that each carried what looked like lethal and very nontraditional submachine guns.

"Deke, do you remember the last time my father's men welcomed you?" Kahil asked.

"Sure do. I spit out sand for a week."

"Prepare for another mouth full. You had better wait with Fahranna, Jaci."

She didn't argue. Those charging camels looked like they meant business.

Kahil put the Land Rover in Park and left the engine idling while he and Deke walked forward twenty or so yards. Hands on hips, they waited for the reception committee.

It arrived in a storm of sand and noise. Whooping and firing their weapons in short, ear-battering bursts, the four riders raced around Kahil and Deke in dizzying circles. Their camels' hooves thundered against the earth. Dust funneled and spun like whirling dervishes.

Jaci had to lean over the front seat to be heard above the clamor. "Is this how they normally greet guests?"

"Only the son of their sheik."

The tumultuous welcome went on for another few minutes. Then the riders reined in their mounts and threw themselves out of the saddle. After much back-pounding and cheek-kissing, Kahil loped back to the Land Rover. Fahranna rolled down the window so he could lean in.

"You don't mind driving down to the oasis, do you?"

"Have I ever?"

"That, my precious pearl, is why you hold my heart."

"Go," she said, laughing, "before the prospect of spending time under your father's roof makes me put this car in Reverse and scurry back to Cairo."

"Ha! You know you love nothing more than pulling his whiskers."

He gave her a grin and a quick kiss before rejoining the reception committee. Two of the riders had doubled up, leaving their camels for Kahil and Deke. They mounted and took off amid more raucous bursts of gunfire.

"Men!" Shaking her head, Fahranna invited Jaci to join her in the front seat.

"Well?" she asked when her passenger had gathered her skirts and scrambled over the gear shift. "Are you ready to beard the lion of the desert in his den?"

"As ready as I'll ever be."

* * *

Lion, Jaci decided, perfectly described Sheik Yousef El Hassan when he strode out of a sprawling, two-story mud-brick house to welcome his daughter-in-law and her guest. Although his beard was snow-white and the desert sun had tanned his skin into a mass of leathery wrinkles, he stood as tall and broad-shouldered as his son. Even more intimidating, he didn't speak. He roared.

He greeted Fahranna with a bellow and a fierce affection that she returned in equal measure. His greeting to Jaci was more restrained but no less thunderous.

"Welcome to Jawal," he boomed in heavily accented English, raking her with a keen eye. "May the blessings of Allah be with you while you reside within my house."

"Thank you."

"You will go with the women to refresh yourself. Then we will speak of this matter that has brought you here."

Fahranna had told Jaci that Kahil's mother had died giving birth to him and his father had never remarried. That didn't mean there was a lack of females at the oasis, however. Along with the sheik and the male members of his extended family, Kahil's aunts, cousins and nieces had all poured out to welcome the newcomers.

Chattering with excitement and delight, the women escorted the new arrivals through a set of double doors studded with brass spikes. Jaci didn't understand a word, but their friendliness and hospitality required no translation.

Almost before she'd stepped into a palm-shaded courtyard, an elderly woman draped in black had pressed a glass of cinnamon-spiced tea into her hand. A younger woman with merry eyes and an impish smile offered a plate of almonds and fresh dates. Chattering a mile a minute, she trailed Jaci up a set of stairs that led to a second story lined with arches.

"She wishes to know if you are promised to al Shamshir," Fahranna translated.

"Al Shamshir?"

"It's an ancient word for scimitar. Sheik Yousef bestowed the name on Deke because his eyes are the color of Damascus steel. And, I suspect, because of the skill with which he wields a weapon."

Jaci had an all-too-vivid memory of Deke wielding his weapon. Both of his weapons!

"Please tell her I'm not promised to al Shamshir."

She had no idea what Fahranna said, but it resulted in a burst of laughter from the other women. They were still giggling when they ushered Jaci into a high-ceilinged chamber. The first thing that struck her was the blessedly cool air. She assumed the shuttered windows and four-foot thick walls accounted for that until Fahranna pointed to three vents in the ceiling.

"Heat rises, so the higher opening in the center conducts hot air out. The two smaller openings draw fresh air in."

Whatever. All Jaci knew was that the room was dim and cool and outfitted with a fascinating blend of palm wood furniture and striped Bedouin wall hangings. And it had a shower! Piped in, Fahranna explained, from one of the dozen or so freshwater springs that fed the oasis.

"I'll come for you in a few minutes, after you have had time to refresh yourself. Then we'll go down and join our men."

Jaci didn't bother to correct her use of the possessive. From the unsubtle comments Fahranna had let drop, it was clear she thought the two Americans had more going on between them than foiling an antigovernment conspiracy.

So, apparently, did Sheik Yousef. That became apparent when he granted his daughter-in-law and Jaci the rare privilege of eating with the men of his household.

"Sit there," he boomed, stabbing an imperious forefinger at an empty spot beside Deke. "You will fill your belly first, then you will tell me of this ancient scarab your man says you have found."

A quick glance from "her man" warned her not to contradict the sheik in front of the others. Gathering her robes, Jaci sank onto the low bench beside Deke while Fahranna did the same beside Kahil.

Deke used the tip of a small curved knife to spear chunks of meat from a large clay platter into a bowl. He then scooped up pea risotto and what looked like stuffed beet leaves. When he deposited the bowl in front of her, Jaci glanced around surreptitiously. Nope, no forks or spoons anywhere in sight.

"Like this," Deke murmured.

Following his lead, she picked up another small knife and skewered a chunk of meat. She wasn't sure what it was. Not lamb, she decided after the first bite. Goat, she guessed, boiled in milk to tenderize it before being seared over an open flame.

The risotto proved a little trickier to manage until she once again followed Deke's example and scooped the starchy mixture up with two fingers.

"Now," Sheik Yousef announced when she'd emptied her bowl, washed her hands in warm water and downed a third glass of cinnamon tea, "show me this scarab you have found."

"This is only a replica." Reaching under her scarf, she unclasped the thin gold chain. "The real one is in the custody of the director of the Cairo Museum."

She dropped the beetle in his thorny palm. He fingered it, turning it over to study the markings while Jaci launched into a description of how she'd stumbled at the City of the Dead and the incidents that followed—including Mrs. Grimes's initial assumption she'd been the target of a kidnap attempt by white slavers. The story sounded fantastic even to her own ears.

When she finished, Kahil described the electronic chatter her find had generated and the scarab's subsequent authentication by experts at the Cairo Museum.

Stroking the beetle, the Lion of the Desert skewered Deke with a piercing stare. "And you, al Shamshir? What is your part in all this?"

"My government sent me to assist Kahil in determining whether Jaci had any idea of the hornet's nest she'd stumbled into."

"She did not?"

"No," Deke replied.

"She does now, however."

"She does indeed. That's why I'm here, to protect her."

The sheik's dark eyes lanced from Deke to Jaci and back again.

"It strikes me that may not be the only reason you are here. Just remember, my friend. While this woman is under my roof, she has *my* protection."

It didn't take Jaci long to appreciate how all-encompassing the sheik's protection was.

Of necessity, Bedouin women enjoyed a considerable degree of independence. The harsh, unforgiving desert dictated an equality of labor and movement denied to many of their sisters in more conservative communities. Yet because of Jaci's special circumstances, either Deke or Kahil or a specially designated guard accompanied her every time she departed Yousef El Hassan's home.

One of those guards pulled sentry duty outside the mud-brick dwelling Fahranna used as a clinic. His machine gun tucked in his crossed arms, he waited patiently while Jaci assisted the doctor as best she could.

A similarly armed Deke accompanied her to the small but thriving market the following afternoon, where he helped her bargain for baskets and shawls woven in traditional Bedouin designs for friends at home.

Evenings she spent mostly with the women of the sheik's extended household. After that first night, she and Fahranna weren't invited to dine with the men. Instead, they took their meals in the dining area reserved for women. Lit by oil lamps and noisy with laughter and talk, it was a lively, convivial place.

Ditto her sleeping quarters. As it turned out, Jaci's room was located in the wing reserved for the unmarried females. Oil lamps flickered late into the night as the women sewed or read or conveyed to their guest through pantomime and elaborate hand gestures how lucky she was to have such a man as al Shamshir as her guardian.

She didn't argue. It didn't do any good, given Deke's self-appointed role as guardian and protector. She had to admit he looked the part, too. Adopting local customs, he protected his head and neck from the sun with a traditional Bedouin headdress anchored by thick ropes. His tan deepened to bronzed oak, and the beginnings of a beard darkened his cheeks and chin.

He appeared as fierce as any of the sheik's warriors when he strode into the courtyard the morning of their third day at the oasis. Jaci was bouncing a curly haired toddler on her knee, with a half dozen women clustered around her. Deke immediately snagged every female eye, hers included.

"Kahil just got a radio call from his aide," he told her, his eyes glinting. "The subtle hints Kahil had his people drop have taken root. According to intercepted emails and tweets, Ma'at's true believers know you're at Jawal. They've been trying to decide what to do next."

"How long is Kahil going to let them stew?"

"As long as it takes." His steely gaze locked with hers. "Unless you change your mind and let me hustle you onto a plane back to the States."

"I'm smack in the middle of an empty desert, guarded night and day by heavily armed watchdogs. With," she reminded him, "an entire squadron of air commandos just a radio call away. I might as well see this through."

His mouth set. He wanted to say more. That much was obvious to both Jaci and the women sitting around her. They stopped their various tasks and observed the byplay with unabashed interest.

"We still need to talk about what happened at your hotel," he reminded her.

"No, we don't."

Her response was automatic, but she knew he was right. They needed to talk. She'd had sufficient time in the past few days to work through her anger at his duplicity. She still had a way to go before she could get past her own starry-eyed gullibility. This was hardly the time or the place to bare those emotions, however.

Deke recognized that, as well. He glanced at

the other women in the courtyard. They didn't understand his words, but Jaci knew they were recording every gesture, every inflection, for dissection later.

"Kahil says Fahranna wants to go to the mud baths this afternoon," Deke informed her gruffly. "I'll escort you, and we'll talk then."

Jaci had no idea what one wore to a mud bath. When she asked Fahranna, the physician shrugged.

"You wear nothing."

"'Scuse me?"

"Don't worry. There are separate chambers for men and women. We will strip off all our clothing and wallow in the green Egyptian mud like Nile hippos."

"Sounds, uh, lovely."

"It is," Fahranna replied, laughing. "You won't believe what the mud does for your pores. But it's even more lovely when you rinse off under the stars in a pool fed by a clear, bubbling spring. The baths are the main reason I let Kahil drag me to his father's house."

"If you say so."

Kahil and Deke were waiting when the women went downstairs later that afternoon. Jaci wasn't particularly reassured by the holsters buckled low on their hips. Or the semiautomatic rifles each man had slung across his shoulder. All they needed, she thought, were crossed bandoliers to make her turn tail and scurry back to the women's quarters.

She sneaked a hand under her head scarf and nervously fingered the substitute scarab. The fact that Fahranna also sported a pistol strapped to her hip didn't do much for Jaci's peace of mind.

"The baths are on the other side of the oasis," Kahil said by way of explanation. "Still well within the innermost ring of my father's perimeter defenses. Ordinarily we would not go armed, but given the circumstances Deke and I thought it best to keep weapons close at hand."

When they walked through the heavy double doors, Jaci was still trying to figure out how the men would hang on to all those weapons while rolling around in green Egyptian mud. The sight of a stable boy holding the reins of four kneeling camels brought her to a dead stop.

"Uh-oh." Her expression turned nervous. "I'm not very good at riding one of those," she confessed to Kahil.

"Deke told us." Hiding a smile, he patted a long, hairy neck. "This is one of my father's gentlest milk camels. I've had them mount a child's saddle on her for you. It's smaller and lighter, and the pommels are closer together for a safer ride. You can't fall out."

"I wouldn't bet on that."

Jaci mounted gingerly and hung on while Deke arranged the folds of her robe so they padded her calves against the coarse saddle blanket. He then swung a leg over the saddle of the camel next to hers. Fahranna mounted with the ease of long practice and accepted a cloth sack from Kahil, which she hooked around the pommel.

"Tea and sesame cakes," she told Jaci. "For after we bathe."

It took ten precarious, swaying minutes before Jaci finally loosened her death grip on the reins. Five minutes more before she allowed herself to relax and enjoy the experience of plodding around a salt-rimmed lake while the sun dropped toward the shallow pool at its top.

The late-afternoon sun, Fahranna informed her after they'd slathered mud all over each other and stretched out on stone slabs in the open-air women's cubicle, was necessary to bake the mud into one's pores.

And bake it did! By the time she rolled off the slab, Jaci felt as though she'd been trussed, seasoned and steamed in a clay casserole. Stiff-legged, she followed Fahranna to the natural rock pool. It was fed by a spring that seeped through porous limestone and dropped in a silvery waterfall.

Gasping at the water's unexpected chill, she sank up to her neck and dunked her head repeatedly.

Once she got the mud off her hair and face, she discovered Fahranna was right. Her pores were so tight that her skin felt like glass.

"Wow! I'd like to bottle some of this stuff and carry it home with me."

"You can bottle the mud," the Egyptian said as she floated lazily on her back, "but not our desert sun."

The sound of splashing and the low murmur of voices carried over the wall separating the bathing areas. Resolutely, Jaci tried not to visualize Deke floating on *his* back.

"We'll have tea and sweet cakes with the men after the sun goes down," Fahranna advised. "Seeing the stars light up the night sky here, with no city lights to diffuse their brilliance, is something you'll never forget."

They would take tea and watch the stars come out. Then, Jaci thought, she and Deke would talk.

She waited until they'd demolished the tea and sticky-sweet sesame cakes and the sky had darkened to walk the pool's edge with him.

Jaci could have easily let herself get swept up in their magic if not for her nervousness about the conversation to come. Fahranna kept insisting Deke felt something more than a professional sense of responsibility toward her. She would have loved to believe that. Common sense dictated otherwise. There was nothing in her life—nothing in *her*—that would hold the interest of an adventurer like him. Not for long, anyway.

"Okay." She came to a halt and turned to face him, determined to get it over with. "You wanted to talk. So talk."

He stared down at her, his features shadowed. "First, I need to apologize. I've never…that is, I always…"

He stopped, blew out a breath. Was this smooth, sophisticated, take-charge Deke Griffin? Fumbling for words? His uncharacteristic uncertainty filled Jaci with both surprise and satisfaction.

"Let me help you out here," she said, oozing a sweetness she was far from feeling. "You've already stated unequivocally that making love to me wasn't part of your plan. I believe your exact words were that taking me to bed went against all your training and instincts."

"It did."

"Now you're feeling guilty and a misplaced sense of responsibility for the naive twit you played like a cheap violin."

"That's not what…"

"It's okay, Deke. Really. I've worked through my embarrassment and anger. I've decided to consider the memory of our night together as one more souvenir to take home from my vacation."

"You've decided I'm a *souvenir?*"

"Not the kind I usually collect," she admitted with a halfhearted smile. "I'll have to figure out how to work you into my scrapbook."

Judging by the way his brows snapped together, her attempt at a joke fell completely flat.

"The point is," she said with painful honesty, "you don't have to feel guilty or responsible or this misplaced sense of protectiveness toward me. I might not have known who you were when I invited you into my hotel room, but I did invite you. What happened was as much my fault as it was yours."

"Got it all figured out, have you?"

"I think so."

"Well, I'm damned if I do," he said gruffly.

"'Scuse me?"

"The fact is I *do* feel guilty and responsible and a fierce sense of protectiveness for you. I've also spent more hours than I should have the past few days thinking of ways to get you into bed again."

His hand came up and cupped her cheek.

"I can't do it here, Jaci. Not without risking castration by Sheik Yousef," he added drily. "But I'm going to do my damnedest to make it happen as soon as I get you home safe."

Well! So much for her carefully rehearsed

speech. The man had just made mincemeat of it. And knocked her breath back down her throat in the process.

"In the meantime," he said, his voice husky, "this will have to hold me."

When his lips molded to hers, Jaci realized it would have to hold her, too.

Especially after the rattle of gunfire split the night.

Chapter 11

The shots brought Kahil and Fahranna on the run. They skidded to a halt beside the two Americans, listening intently as short, staccato bursts echoed across the desert. Stark silence followed for five or six seconds.

Jaci's heart jackhammered against her ribs. "What...?"

Three additional bursts cut her off. She almost jumped out of her skin again, but the others visibly relaxed.

"That's my father's signal," Kahil explained. "He wishes us to return."

"What's wrong?" she wanted to know as they

made for their patiently waiting camels. "Why did he signal?"

"We'll know soon enough."

Since the radio clipped to the colonel's belt hadn't broadcast an alarm, Jaci figured she didn't need to worry. Yet an uneasy feeling seemed to seep into her with each thud of her camel's hooves. Although she knew the scarab dangling on its thin gold chain was a fake, the urge to touch it grew too powerful to ignore. Awkwardly, she gathered her mount's reins in one hand and slipped the other under the veil she'd hurriedly draped across her head and throat.

When they arrived at the main house, Sheik Yousef met them in the vestibule. "A vehicle approaches," he announced in his thunderous bass.

"Only one?" his son asked.

"Only one. My sentries have tracked it for the past half hour."

That didn't sound like an invasion of the body snatchers to Jaci. Yet her nerves crawled as she waited with the others. Nervously, she clutched her substitute scarab. She didn't understand why the heck it gave her such comfort but it did.

What seemed like an eternity later, one of the sheik's men escorted a dusty—but very familiar—figure into the house.

"Hanif!"

The tour guard looked exhausted. He was wearing his standard uniform—the dark green suit with the jacket cut loosely enough to accommodate the compact submachine gun that bulged under the back flap—but it was his grim expression that sent a shiver of dread down Jaci's spine.

"What are you doing here? What's happened?"

"Your friend, Mrs. Grimes. She's had an accident."

Jaci gasped. "Oh, no! What kind of an accident?"

"She was hit by a taxi while crossing the street."

"Dear God! Is she badly hurt?"

"She is in the hospital. The doctors say her condition is very critical." The guard's dark eyes held hers. "She asks for you. My supervisor at the agency, he tries to call you but the call does not go through on your cell phone. So I drive to Jawal to tell you."

Jaci might be naive and a tad clumsy but she was no fool. A thread of doubt wove its way through her shock and dismay. Instinctively, she turned to Deke.

He had the same doubts, she saw. His face was set and his eyes cool, but before either he or Kahil could question Hanif, Fahranna took charge.

"What hospital is she in?" the physician asked the tour guard briskly.

"Dar al Fouad."

"That's one of our best," she assured Jaci. "It's critical care unit is world renowned. Kahil, get on your radio and contact your command center. Have them patch me through to the doctor in charge of the CCU."

The eyes of everyone in the room locked on the colonel as he unhooked the radio from his belt and keyed the mike. After a burst of static, someone answered and Kahil barked out a rapid order. While they waited for the connection, Hanif turned to Jaci.

"Your tour group leaves tomorrow for Luxor. I must go with them. It is my job. But it worries me that your friend will have no one except a representative from the tour agency with her."

Jaci caught her lower lip between her teeth. Susan Grimes had watched over her like a mother hen. The possibility that the kind, gregarious woman might lie in the hospital for days or weeks with no family or friends beside her bed made Jaci throw a desperate glance at Deke.

His expression remained impassive, but she could guess what he was thinking. Had the so-called true believers turned the tables on them? Were they using Susan Grimes as bait for the bait? Was Hanif one of them?

Not only possible, Jaci thought with a sudden

lurch in her stomach, but very probable. The guard was the only Egyptian she'd shown Ma'at's scarab to the day she found it. Not long afterward, Egyptian authorities had begun picking up suspicious phone and email chatter.

Fahranna's terse exchange with the doctor at the hospital cut into her whirling thoughts. Since it was conducted in Arabic, she held her breath until the physician handed the radio back to her husband.

"It's as he says," she told Jaci gravely. "Your friend sustained massive trauma to the head and is in very critical condition."

Stricken by the news, Jaci didn't hesitate. "I need to get back to Cairo immediately."

"I will drive you." Hanif's glance shifted to the man beside her. "And any other who wishes to go."

She caught the quick look Deke and Kahil exchanged. So did Sheik Yousef.

"The sands can be treacherous at night," the Lion of the Desert reminded them. "My men and I will escort you."

"No need," his son replied, once again keying his radio mike. "I'll call in a chopper."

Hanif opened his mouth, then snapped it shut again. He stood as stiff and silent as the others until the colonel signed off.

"The chopper will be here in ten minutes."

The announcement clearly startled the tour guard. "How is it possible for a helicopter to arrive from Cairo so quickly?"

"The crew is part of a unit performing night exercises not far from here," Kahil replied smoothly. "They're diverting here to pick me up. Jaci, you will want to gather your things."

She rushed toward the stairs. Fahranna came with her, as did several of the women who'd gathered downstairs to check out the unexpected visitor. They helped her shove the items she'd bought at the souk and the few belongings she brought with her into her carryall.

"Please," she implored Fahranna, "tell them how grateful I am for their friendliness and hospitality. I will send thank-you gifts as soon as I can."

"You don't need to send gifts."

"I know, but I want to," she insisted.

Sheik Yousef said the same when Jaci thanked him. Folding her hands between both of his calloused palms, he boomed down at her.

"All that is necessary is that you see your friend through her injury. And that you return to Jawal for another visit someday."

"I would love to."

The cackle of his son's radio turned all heads. When Kahil once again reached under his billowing robe, everyone present—including Hanif—got a good view of the holster strapped to his hip.

"The chopper is on final approach," the colonel advised his tense listeners. "I told them we would use the lights from our vehicles to guide them to a safe LZ."

"Then we'd better get to it," Deke bit out.

"I will help," Hanif said, "then I will drive back to Cairo."

Deke and Kahil didn't so much as glance at each other this time, but Jaci picked up on their unspoken signals. They were both reserving judgment on the guard and this seemingly legit emergency. After another flurry of goodbyes, Jaci and Fahranna accompanied the men through the brass-studded doors and out into the night.

Mere minutes later, Kahil pulled the Land Rover up on a long finger of hard-baked mudflats that ran well clear of the date palms. He left the engine running and the lights on. Hanif did the same on the opposite side of the flats.

The crossed beams of their headlights vectored the helicopter in. Its powerful searchlight skimmed the area, blinding the watchers during its approach. The *whap-whap-whap* of the rotor blades was deafening. Kahil had to shout into his radio to give them clearance to touch down.

As the chopper slowly descended, the bite of

sand thrown up by its blades proved ten times worse than the noise. Gasping, Jaci dragged her scarf across her face and squinted at the whirling sand.

It obscured almost everything. She could barely make out Deke as he reached back inside the Land Rover for their overnight bags, or Hanif, when he plowed across the flats with an arm flung across his face to protect it.

"I will see you at the hospital in Cairo," he shouted.

Jaci nodded, her doubts about him allayed by the presence of the helicopter and their imminent departure.

"Thank you for driving all this way to tell me about Mrs. Grimes," she shouted back.

"What?"

"I said *thank you*."

Hanif shook his head, pointed to his ear and moved closer. Jaci squinted at the man through the slit in her veil. She had difficulty seeing him through the slinging sand, but the sudden, fiercely intense look in his eyes sent a fission down her spine. Before she could do more than take a step back, he'd leaped forward, thrust a hand under her veil and buried a hand in her hair. The next instant something hard and small and round jammed into her ribs.

The snake-fast attack caught the others by surprise. Deke wasn't more than three or four feet away. He spun in a half circle, then froze as Hanif shouted a warning.

"If you reach for your weapons, I will kill her!"

"Ma'at's messenger?" Deke yelled back, every muscle in his body taut. "You'll kill Ma'at's messenger?"

"If I must!"

He tightened his savage hold on Jaci's hair. Fiery pain tore at her scalp. She thrust up both hands in an agony to ease his grip but couldn't reach under the head cloth now dragged tight against her throat. With one frantic hand, she tugged at the choking fabric. The other tangled in the scarab's thin gold chain.

Some good luck charm! The hysterical thought shot through her as Hanif bellowed at the others, almost shattering her eardrum.

"The true believers cannot allow Ma'at's messenger to fall into the hands of this corrupt government. They will use her to distort the goddess's message."

Tears stung Jaci's eyes and blurred the tableau that would remain etched indelibly in her mind for the rest of her life.

However long that was!

Deke gripped the carryalls in white-knuckled fists. His jaw was locked and murder flamed in his eyes. Kahil had stepped in front of Fahranna to shield her with his body. Behind them, the side hatch of the helicopter had slid open. A crewman in a zippered air force flight suit squinted out at the group gathered beside the Land Rover.

He couldn't see what was happening, Jaci realized in desperation. They were standing outside the spear of the headlights. Even with the reflected glare from the chopper's landing and cockpit lights, her flowing robe hid the weapon jammed into her ribs, and her head scarf covered Hanif's brutal grip on her hair.

"Your radio!" Hanif shouted to Kahil above the undulating whine of the engines. "Unclip it and throw it on the ground here, by me!"

The colonel spit out something in Egyptian that made Hanif's fist jerk and almost tore Jaci's hair out by the roots. When tears poured down her contorted face, Deke snarled at his friend.

"Throw down the damned radio!"

Kahil's primary means of communicating with his troops slammed onto mud baked to concrete hardness. Hanif shoved Jaci two steps ahead of him.

His boot heel came down on the radio. She didn't hear it smash above the engine's earsplitting drone, but she saw the muscle jump in the side of Deke's jaw when Hanif pushed her toward the chopper.

They took another step. And another. Deke's eyes never left her face. She could read their message despite the whirling sand and her blinding tears of pain.

Go with him.

Don't do anything stupid.

I'll find you.

She wanted to believe him. *Had* to believe him. She signaled her understanding as her scrabbling, clutching fingers closed around the scarab. It was fake. She knew it was fake. Yet she clutched the beetle so tightly that its single antenna gouged deep into her palm. Unbidden, her mind sent a frantic prayer winging into the night.

Listen up, Ma'at. If you're anywhere in the vicinity, this would be a great time to kick some butt.

She couldn't move her head, could hardly breathe, but from the corner of one eye she saw the crewman leaning out of the hatch. Frowning, the airman beckoned to his would-be passengers. He still couldn't see the gun at Jaci's back. He must have begun to suspect something was wrong, though, as he jumped down onto the skid and started across the hard-packed flats.

Jaci felt rather than saw Hanif half turn toward

the man. The gun barrel moved with him, its tip
vicious as it scraped along her rib. For a mere second, it cleared her side and poked at the folds of
her robe.

She didn't stop to think, didn't weigh the odds.
She knew she had less than a heartbeat to act.
Sobbing with fear and utter desperation, she angled
the scarab's head through her middle and third
finger and closed her fist around the hard malachite
of its body. Knuckles clenched, she swung with
everything in her.

Her fist connected with a thud. Liquid spurted
over Jaci's head and face.

Howling like a wounded animal, Hanif reacted
instinctively. His submachine gun spit fire and
cordite. The acrid stink burned Jaci's nostrils.
Bullets ripped through the folds of her robe as he
released his brutal grip on her hair and slapped his
free hand to his face.

His violent gyrations threw her sideways. She
sensed rather than saw Deke throw himself at her
attacker. Shoved clear of the two men, she hit the
ground with a jarring thud. Her legs tangled in her
long skirt as she fought to roll out of the way of
the men who suddenly crashed down beside her.
Hanif fired off several long, lethal bursts, but Deke
managed to keep the barrel pointed at the star-
studded sky. Then Kahil delivered a soccer kick

that splintered the bones in the guard's arm. His weapon spun off into the darkness. His screams of pain ricocheted through the night.

Only after Deke pushed to his feet and helped Jaci up did she see the blood gushing through the fingers Hanif had splayed over his right eye. A half inch or so of her fake beetle, she saw with a sickening lurch in her belly, protruded between his fingers. Her frantic swing had thrust the gold antenna deep into the man's eyeball.

After that, things seemed to happen at the speed of light.

Relieved at their close escape but appalled by the damage she'd inflicted on another human being, Jaci barely heard Kahil shout something to the chopper's crew chief.

He rushed to the cockpit, gesturing wildly to explain what had happened to the pilot and copilot while Fahranna knelt beside Hanif to assess his condition. Even with Deke holding the man down, he screamed and writhed too violently for Fahranna to help him until Kahil retrieved her medical bag from the Land Rover. With swift efficiency, she broke a capsule of some kind of painkiller—morphine, Jaci guessed—and jabbed the needle right through Hanif's pants into his thigh. It must have been a powerful dose. Within seconds, the guard's screams dwindled to moans and Fahranna was able to pry his hand away from his face.

"I can't do anything for him here," she announced after a quick and very grim examination. "We have to fly him to a hospital. Get him aboard."

While Hanif was being carried to the chopper, Sheik Yousef and a half dozen of his men came thundering across the desert with their weapons at the ready. Kahil gave them a swift explanation of the gunfire before joining his wife, Deke and Jaci in the chopper's hold. As soon as the colonel had strapped himself in, the crew chief handed him a headset. Moments later, the aircraft lifted off.

Hot air whipped in through the open hatch. Jaci was wedged between Deke and Fahranna, strapped tight in a web seat, but she got a good view of Jawal when the chopper tipped into a steep bank. For an instant or two, the oasis was right below her. The palms fringing the water looked like feather dusters, surrounded as far as she could see by undulating mounds of silvery sand. And there, in the distance, the darker silhouettes of the mud-brick dwellings, their windows lit with the flickering glow of lamplight.

When the helicopter pulled out of its steep turn, she put Jawal out of sight and out of mind. From that point on, regret for the awful injury she'd inflicted on Hanif warred with a growing, gnawing worry over Susan Grimes.

Jaci's breath snagged at the sight of her friend hooked up to a stomach-clenching array of monitors and drip bags. The retired schoolteacher looked terrifyingly like an Egyptian mummy. Bandages swathed her entire head, with only small openings for her eyes, nose and mouth. But when Jaci gently took her hand and murmured her name, Susan's lashes fluttered up.

It took several seconds for recognition to dawn. When it did, her fingers spasmed. She attempted to speak, but all she could manage was a low, hoarse croak.

"Don't try to talk," Jaci whispered, her throat tight. "Just rest. I'm here. So is Deke. We'll stay with you."

She spoke from her heart, not really thinking. Only belatedly did she remember that Deke had completed his assigned task. He'd verified that she wasn't part of the antigovernment conspiracy. He'd also helped neutralize the threat. Kahil could wring the names of the other conspirators out of Hanif. No need for him to hang around any longer.

Yet he reinforced her reckless promise with a nod. "We'll stay as long as you need us," he confirmed gruffly.

The hand Jaci was holding spasmed again. With

an effort that was painful to observe, Susan Grimes croaked out three whispered words.

"Someone...pushed...me."

Gentle, tenderhearted Jaci felt a flash of white-hot fire in her veins. The wrath of a vengeful goddess fueled a fury like none she'd ever known. If it wasn't Hanif who'd shoved Susan in front of an oncoming taxi to lure Ma'at's messenger away from her protectors, it had to be one of his co-conspirators.

Jaci damned every one of them with the depths of her soul.

Chapter 12

Jaci spent most of the next forty-eight hours at the hospital. The sight of pale-colored scrubs and beeping monitors became as familiar to her as the scent of antiseptic. Despite Deke's concern for her safety and Fahranna's assurance that she would personally attend to Mrs. Grimes, Jaci refused to leave Susan's side until the schoolteacher was taken off the critical list and moved out of the critical care unit.

The confession Kahil extracted from Hanif registered only on the periphery of her consciousness. Ditto the colonel's frustration at Hanif's stubborn refusal to name his coconspirators. She didn't really focus on anything but Susan's valiant struggle until Deke walked into the hospital room two days after their return from the oasis.

"I contacted our operations center last night," he informed Jaci and a still woozy Susan. "We've set up a special aircraft to fly you both back to the States."

Instant and very palpable relief spread across the older woman's face. "They've been good to me here," she murmured through her bandages. "So good. But I want to go home."

"I know." Carefully, Deke stroked the paper-thin skin above her bandaged wrist. "My associate set everything up. She's piloting the aircraft, in fact. She used to fly medevac missions in and out of Iraq, so you'll be in good hands."

"Thank you."

"You're welcome."

Watching his gentle touch, listening to his deep, calm voice, Jaci knew her knight in shining armor was back up on his charger.

He might never follow up on the husky promise he'd made out there at the oasis, just before Hanif showed on the scene. And she knew in her heart that they lived in different planes. Yet at that moment what she felt for him went deeper than anything she'd ever imagined, much less experienced.

Just as well, she realized a few moments later,

because this might be all she'd ever have of him. She saw it in his eyes as he caught her gaze across Susan's bed and jerked his chin toward the door.

"The pilot who's on this aircraft," he said when they'd gained the hallway. "Her name's Victoria Talbot, code name Rebel. She's acted as my backup on this op."

Jaci's stomach sank. Her instincts had been right. He was handing her off.

"I asked Rebel to fly you out," Deke said, confirming her suspicions. "You and Mrs. Grimes. Once she gets you both home, she'll stay with you until Kahil drags enough names from Hanif to take down the entire nest of 'true believers.'"

"I take it you're going to assist with the inquisition?" she said slowly.

"Yeah, I am." His jaw hardened. "I'm not partial to the idea that one or more of them might decide to follow you back to the States."

She wasn't partial to the idea, either.

"When do Susan and I leave?"

"Rebel just radioed. The evac plane is on final approach to Cairo International as we speak."

That quick! After these long, sleepless hours at the hospital, events suddenly seemed to be taking giant leaps forward.

"Do I have time to say goodbye to Kahil and Fahranna?"

"Fahranna's on her way to the hospital. She'll help prepare Susan for transport. Kahil you'll have to call. He's working the few leads Hanif gave up before he went into surgery."

Jaci wanted to feel sorry for the guard. She really did. She'd never inflicted grievous bodily harm on anyone before. Or minor bodily harm, for that matter.

Then again, she'd never had a gun barrel jammed against her ribs. Or sat at the bedside of a friend who'd been pushed in front of a careening taxi. Those experiences seriously impacted her sympathy factor.

"One more thing," Deke said. "No, two. First, Kahil talked to his friend at the Cairo Museum. They're going to put out the word that additional testing has verified that the scarab you found is a fake crafted in the late-nineteenth century. A clever one, but still a fake. That should take the radicals' focus off you."

"But…"

The protest formed, hot and swift. After so many centuries, it seemed a shame to deny the goddess her due. More than a shame. Almost a sacrilege. Indignant on Ma'at's behalf, Jaci had to voice a protest.

"Declaring the scarab a fake will rob Egypt of a precious piece of her heritage. I'm surprised a venerable institution like the Cairo Museum is willing to go along with the lie."

"The museum relies heavily on government grants and funding," Deke replied with a shrug. "They'll play ball…at least until Kahil rounds up the rest of the players in this crazy game."

Jaci couldn't shake the dogged need to have Ma'at's symbol given the respect it deserved.

"*Then* will the museum validate the scarab as authentic?"

"I suppose. That's not my top priority. I'm more concerned with making sure you're safe. Which brings me to the second item on my list."

When Deke framed her face with his palms and leaned down to cover her lips with his, Jaci banished all thoughts of scarabs and goddesses.

Her response was purely instinctual. Rising up, she hooked her arms around his neck and gave herself up to the feel of his mouth on hers. It washed through her, gentle waves that alternated with rushing heat. She could have lost herself in insidious pleasure. Would have, if the ping of elevator doors and the assured clip of approaching footsteps hadn't penetrated the haze.

"Much as I hate to interrupt," Fahranna said, amusement threading her voice, "I need to know the specifics of the equipment aboard the plane that will transport Jaci and her friend back to the States."

Deke raised his head, and the regret in his eyes mirrored Jaci's. She held that look in her heart through the next hectic hours.

It stayed with her until well after the specially configured medevac aircraft was airborne and winging its way above an achingly blue Mediterranean. Only then, with Susan snoring softly in a drugged sleep and the medical personnel conferring quietly at the front of the plane, did the doubts begin to seep in.

They were so different, she and Deke. Although she craved travel and adventure, she preferred them dished up in easily digestible servings. He lived day after day on a steady diet of both. His aviation consultant business took him to the far corners of the globe. What's more, his work for this secret, shadowy government agency added an edge that fascinated Jaci as much as it intimidated her.

Now here she was, heading back to her comfortable little nest while Deke helped Kahil track down a band of potentially violent conspirators. Nibbling on her lower lip, she stared out the window while tired clichés drifted through in her equally tired brain.

Out of sight, out of mind.

Easy come, easy go.

And the really scary bit about not being able to teach old dogs new tricks.

She was still chewing on that one when the pilot of the aircraft left her copilot at the throttles and exited the cockpit.

"How's our patient?" she asked the medical officer in charge.

"Stable and sleeping."

Nodding, the leggy blonde made her way back to Jaci's seat. "How about you?"

"Stable and wide-awake."

"Ace mentioned in his report that you collected a few bruises before you took out the guy who came after you. The doctor probably has something in his bag of tricks that would ease the aches and help you sleep."

"I'm fine."

"That was nice work, by the way."

"It was more luck than anything else," Jaci acknowledged ruefully.

"Not according to Ace." A smile tugged at the pilot's lips. "You seem to have made quite an impression on him."

"That works both ways." Jaci hesitated. She wasn't the prying type, but this opportunity was too good to pass up. "Have you known him long?"

"Long enough."

It was the blonde's turn to pause. She and Deke

and the others in their supersecret organization lived by a strict code, Jaci guessed. They wouldn't reveal information about the agency's operatives to an outsider. Probably not even to each other. So she was surprised when Talbot treated her to a wry grin.

"I have to admit I'm curious. So is everyone else back at the agency. Ace hasn't requested this level of post-op security for a target before."

"Target?" Jaci echoed with a grimace.

"Person of interest," she amended. "You certainly appear to be that."

There were so many shades of nuance in that comment that Jaci didn't even try to decode them.

"He just wants to keep me under wraps until he and Kahil nose out the rest of the conspirators," she said with a show of nonchalance.

"You think so, huh? I guess we'll see."

"Guess we will," Jaci murmured as the pilot tipped her a two-fingered salute and made her way back to the cockpit.

Susan Grimes' granddaughter was waiting when the jet touched down at Gainesville Regional Airport. A third-year nursing student at the university, Debby had arranged an ambulance and skilled care for her grandmother. She'd also opted to move in with her during her post-hospital recovery. Grandmother and granddaughter greeted each other with such obvious affection that Jaci had no qualms about relinquishing the patient to Debby's care.

The schoolteacher was still dopey but gave Jaci's hand a squeeze before being rolled to the ambulance. "Come see me," she murmured drowsily.

"I will."

"You and Deke."

"He stayed in Cairo," Jaci reminded her. "I'm, uh, not sure when he'll make it to Florida."

When, or if.

Now that she'd returned to familiar surroundings, Jaci's doubts magnified. Suddenly Egypt seemed so far away. Everything that had happened there so unbelievable. She almost pinched herself while she waited for Victoria Talbot to turn the aircraft over to the copilot and collect the vehicle waiting for her at the airport.

As Victoria trailed Jaci through Gainesville's tree-lined streets, Cairo's raucous, bustling traffic and the vast emptiness of the Western Desert seemed to recede further with each turn of the wheels.

Reclaiming her two felines from the friend who'd been pet-sitting them only reinforced the odd feeling of separation. Mittens, lazy slug that she was, could barely be bothered to acknowledge Jaci's return. Lively little Boots went to the opposite extreme. He gave her a number of ecstatic, raspy kisses before scrambling onto her shoulder. Tail swishing, claws dug in, he remained perched there throughout the ride to her condo.

Another friend had checked the place and watered the plants, but the two-bedroom unit still gave off a musty air. Jaci dispelled that with scented oil sticks while Victoria did a walk-through.

The blonde had switched to full operative mode. Watching her in action, Jaci had no difficulty thinking of her in terms of her code name. Precise and efficient, Rebel checked the locks on windows and doors before installing what she termed a very basic intrusion detection system. She then walked through each room, fixing their layout in her mind as she skimmed the ceilings, walls and fixtures with a handheld device.

"What's that?" Jaci asked as she and Mittens followed her through the rooms.

"A handy-dandy bug sniffer, developed by the genius who heads OMEGA's electronics division."

She was looking for listening devices, Jaci realized with a gulp. *Not* the silverfish and palmetto bugs and other pests that invaded Florida homes.

This all, too, seemed so unreal. She couldn't imagine how the conspirators would've had time to bug her cozy condo. Or that they would want to.

"OMEGA's co-opted the empty unit directly across the courtyard from yours," Rebel informed her. "I'll set up operations there."

"The room I use as an office has a sofa bed," Jaci offered while a playful Mittens batted at the other woman's pant leg. "You could stay here."

Rebel shook her head and scooped up the black-and-white fur ball. "You need your space. And, depending on how long it takes Ace to wrap things up in Egypt, I'll need backup for 24/7 surveillance. You don't want strangers camped out indefinitely in your office. But," she added as she scratched behind Mittens's ears, "we'll get to know each other real well in the next days or weeks."

Weeks?

"I'll give you the number at the empty unit," she said over the cat's ecstatic purrs. "Also my cell phone. Contact me before you go out, and I'll either go with you or stay right on your tail. Ditto if anything makes you nervous. Anything at all."

Ooo-kay.

"When do you plan to go back to work?"

Frowning, Jaci counted time zones and hospital days. They'd all run together in her mind. It took her several moments to sort through them and recognize that this was Thursday afternoon.

"I'm not expected back until the middle of next week," she said with a twinge of regret for her shortened vacation. "I'll probably go in on Monday, though."

"Wise move to wait a few days. You'll need that time to recover from jet lag."

Among other things. Like almost getting kidnapped. Being whisked off to a desert oasis. Having the hottest, most intense sex of her life. *And* losing her heart to a certain consultant/secret agent.

She looked around, taking in the plants and fluffy throw pillows, and tried to convince herself it wasn't all a hallucination. Especially that incredibly erotic sex with the man of her dreams. Gulping, she wrenched her attention back to Rebel and the ecstatically vibrating Mittens.

"Before I crash, I want to hit the grocery store and pick up my mail from the post office."

"That works for me," the agent said. "I can stock up on a few things, as well."

"Oh! I belong to an Ancient Civilizations study group. It meets tonight."

Rebel shot her a quick glance. "Isn't that the group that includes Dr. Nasif Abdouh?"

"You know about him?" Jaci asked curiously.

"Ace had me check him out." Her hand stilled, precipitating a protesting mewl from the cat draped over her arm. "He didn't tell you Abdouh has been funneling funds to an antigovernment dissent group in Egypt?"

"No, he didn't."

Good grief! Talk about guilt by association! No wonder she'd come under such scrutiny. As if that business with the scarab weren't suspicious enough.

"I had no idea," Jaci exclaimed. "Honestly!"

"It didn't take Ace long to reach the same conclusion," Rebel assured her. "Otherwise…"

Her shrug said it all. Otherwise Jaci might well be sitting in an Egyptian jail cell at this very moment.

Or be arrested while trying to flee the country. Like Dr. Abdouh.

She heard about it as soon as she clicked on her answering machine to check the phone messages that had piled up in her absence. Three different members of her study group had called to relay the astounding news.

His arrest was apparently still the main topic of conversation when Jaci walked into the meeting that evening. She heard his name mentioned and the wild speculation being tossed around when she and Rebel appeared at the door. Her appearance was almost as much of a surprise.

"Jaci! What are you doing here?"

"Weren't you supposed to be in Egypt for another week?"

"What happened?"

She couldn't tell them the real story, as fantastic as it was. Not until Ace or Rebel gave her the green light. So she stuck to the simple truth.

"Some of you may know Susan Grimes, a member of my tour group. She was in an accident and had to be airlifted home. I accompanied her back to the States."

After murmurs of sympathy and inquiries into Susan's condition, the group shifted its attention to Rebel. Jaci explained her presence with another truth.

"Victoria piloted the plane that ferried us home. She's staying over for a few days…"

Or weeks.

"…So I invited her to join us tonight."

That satisfied the group, since they were all eager to return to the subject of Dr. Abdouh's arrest. Jaci pleaded ignorance but listened with intense interest to the sketchy details the group tossed back and forth.

The Thursday-night group set the pattern for the encounters that followed.

The members of Beethoven's study group expressed the same surprise when Jaci appeared at their monthly conclave Saturday afternoon. So did her fellow librarians when she showed for work Monday morning.

Rebel begged off attending the cat lovers' coffee

klatch Tuesday evening. Instead, she dropped her charge at the designated meeting place with instructions to contact her when the group was about to disperse.

As the meeting broke up, Jaci used her hostess's phone to place the required call. But when she walked into the balmy Florida night, she saw at a glance it wasn't a long-legged female leaning against the front fender of a rental. The leanee was several inches taller, more broad shouldered and most definitely male.

Her heart gave a joyous leap…and quickly clunked back into place. While she struggled with wrenching disappointment, the stranger pushed away from the fender.

"Hi, Jaci. I'm Clint Black. Rebel's relief. I just got in a little while ago. She had some urgent business to take care of and asked me to pick you up."

Jaci had learned her lesson in Egypt. She backed up a step and kept the front door handle firmly in her grip. "How do I know you're who you say you are?"

"Check your cell phone. You must have turned it off. Rebel left both a text message and a voice mail."

She flipped up her phone. Sure enough, she'd put the thing on silent mode at the start of the coffee klatch. The display showed one voice and one text messages, both from Rebel. But the information that an operative nicknamed "Blade" would pick her up didn't prove particularly reassuring.

Rebel's associate didn't appear to live up to his assigned code name, however. His smile invited trust, and his manner remained easygoing and loose during the drive home. Jaci found herself relaxing in his engaging company…right up until he turned onto her street and they spotted a vehicle parked a little way from her condo.

Their headlights speared through the darkened windows. Jaci thought she caught the gleam of honey-gold hair in the driver's seat. Her sudden tension eased, then shot off the charts again when the passenger door opened.

Chapter 13

"Deke!"

Jaci shouldered her door open even before Blade hit the brakes. The car was sliding to a stop when she jumped out. The combination of forward momentum, soaring excitement and her habitual klutziness made her trip over her own feet.

As he had at the pyramids of Giza, Deke leaped across the short distance separating them. He caught her just as she went down and cradled her against his chest. His eyes gleaming in the light of the blazing headlights, he grinned down at her.

"Is this going to become a habit?"

As *she* had at the pyramids, Jaci reveled in the strength of his arms. "I sincerely hope so."

A car door slammed behind her, and Blade's acerbic comment penetrated through her haze of happiness.

"You might have let me know you intended to deliver Ace here, Rebel."

The reply carried the same sting. "Where did you think I intended to deliver him?"

No love lost there. The thought flitted into Jaci's mind, then flitted right out as Deke's arms tightened around her.

"Sorry Rebel had to call you in on such short notice, Blade. She didn't know I was already in the air, on my way back to the States." He hefted Jaci higher and started for the front door. "You two can shut down operations and head home. I'll take it from here."

"Victoria!" Wiggling up, Jaci called over Deke's shoulder. "Thanks for everything. You, too, er..."

Darned if she could remember his real name.

"Blade."

Then Deke was leaning down so she could insert her key in the lock. Once inside, he dipped again so she could flip on the lights. Her first good look at his face drove his associate's departure right out of her head.

"Have you slept since I left Egypt?" she gasped, shocked by his red-rimmed eyes.

"Not that I remember. But I plan to make up for that real quick. Which way to your bedroom?"

She gestured in the general direction and tried to pry information out of him on the way.

"Deke! You have to tell me! Did Hanif spill the names of the others in the conspiracy? Did Kahil round them up? Is it over? Really over?"

"Yes, yes and yes. Really."

He lowered her to the bed. Jaci scrambled to the side to make room for him but had to know.

"What about Ma'at's scarab? Will the museum folks now validate its authenticity?"

"No clue," he muttered as he took off shoes, shirt and jeans. "I jumped a plane the minute Kahil took the last of Hanif's cohorts into custody."

There were so many other questions Jaci wanted answers to. How many conspirators he and Kahil had rooted out. The reaction, if any, in the Cairo papers to the improbable plot. Hanif's current condition. But the weariness carved into Deke's face put everything else on hold.

It was enough that he was here.

More than enough.

With a tremulous smile, she shed her outer layers of clothing and opened her arms. He sank into them and was out, like, ten seconds later.

She held him, just held him, until the need to

draw a little air into her lungs forced her to wiggle out from under his dead weight.

Jaci wasn't sure how long she lay stretched out beside him, watching him sleep, listening to his heavy breathing, before her lids started to drift down. Twenty minutes? An hour? Long enough for her to give up trying to prevent Mittens and Boots from claiming their usual spots on the bed, anyway. She lost the battle and fell asleep on the sincere hope that Deke wasn't allergic to cat hair.

He wasn't, Jaci discovered happily when she woke the next morning. Boots lay curled in the hollow between their bodies while Deke rubbed his fat, upturned belly. He had all four paws up in the air and an expression of utter bliss on his gray-and-white face.

Jaci's heart melted into soupy mush. If she hadn't already fallen hard for this man, the sight of him tickling her cat's freckled belly would have done the trick. So when he gave her a rueful smile and asked almost the same question he'd asked her last night, she was able to return the same answer.

"This thing with your cats joining us in bed? Is it going to become a habit?"

"I sincerely hope so."

"I don't mind. Much. But we need to set some boundaries."

"We do, huh?" She smirked.

"We do. I don't want to crush Jellybrum here when I make love to you."

Jaci was almost as surprised by the fact that he knew the characters from the long-running musical *Cats* as she was thrilled by the lazy promise.

"Then by all means," she replied on a breathless note, "let me take them into the kitchen. They need to be fed, anyway."

"So do I."

His slow smile sent her stomach into an instant spin. She rolled out of bed wearing only her underwear and hauled the cats to the kitchen with something less than her usual gentleness. Mittens took the rough handling in stride. Boots indicated his displeasure with a twitch of his whiskers and unsheathed claws.

Jaci dodged the sideswipe and dumped cat food into their dishes. While they feasted, she brewed a quick pot of coffee. She slipped out of the kitchen with a steaming mug in each hand and used her hip to nudge the door shut behind her. Every nerve in her body pulsed as she padded back to the bedroom.

Deke had hit the bathroom during her absence. He was back in bed, his shoulders braced against the headboard, but his hair glistened from a damp comb-through, and he'd scrubbed the sleep from his eyes. Wishing she'd had time to do the same,

Jaci watched his gaze do a quick skim of her semi-nude body before locking on the mugs.

"Please tell me that's coffee."

"I thought you could use some."

"You thought right, my luscious goddess."

Preening, she handed him a mug. Luscious wasn't a word she would ever apply to herself. But if Deke thought the adjective fit, why argue?

The goddess bit raised some uneasy questions, however. Like whether she might continue to figure as a player in an ancient legend. And whether some other nut group might decide to track down Ma'at's supposed messenger.

"Not to worry," Deke replied when she voiced the scary thought. "The scarab you found *is* ancient and is most likely made of malachite from King Solomon's mines. But subsequent carbon dating pinned it to at least a century later than the one that would have been buried in Ma'at's temple. Kahil and the director of the Cairo Museum will make sure the word gets out."

Jaci hovered between relief and a thoroughly ridiculous disappointment. "Well, as nerve-racking as it was at times, I have to admit that little scarab added some spice in my otherwise humdrum life."

"Too much spice," Deke said with some feeling.

He set his mug on the nightstand and reached for

hers. Her nerves danced at the brush of his fingers, then did a joyous somersault at the gruff note that came into his voice.

"Last night was the first night I've slept—really slept—since Kahil and I set you up as bait."

"That worried you, did it?"

He combed his fingers through her hair. "Like you wouldn't believe."

"Try me," Jaci said softly.

He gently tugged a hank of hair to bring her down to his level. "You want me to say it?"

"Well…yes."

"Okay, here it is. I love you."

Jaci waited. Five seconds. Ten.

"That's it?"

"Isn't that enough?" he asked, honestly perplexed.

"It's a start."

"What more do you need?"

Not much, she thought ruefully. Just some idea of whether his love was the kind that would lead to something deeper. Like a commitment. Or an engagement. Or, gasp, marriage!

And if it did, which one of them would alter their life to accommodate the other? Where would they live? Would he expect her to sit home and twiddle her thumbs while he jetted off to parts unknown?

But he looked so perplexed that she had to smile.

"I don't need anything more. I love you, too. Now kiss me. Quick. The kitchen won't hold the cats for long."

* * * * *

COMING NEXT MONTH

Available January 25, 2011

#1643 NO ORDINARY HERO
Conard County: The Next Generation
Rachel Lee

#1644 IN HIS PROTECTIVE CUSTODY
The Doctors Pulaski
Marie Ferrarella

#1645 DEADLY VALENTINE
"Her Un-Valentine" by Justine Davis
"The February 14th Secret" by Cindy Dees

#1646 THE PRODIGAL BRIDE
The Bancroft Brides
Beth Cornelison

ROMANTIC SUSPENSE

SRSCNM0111

REQUEST YOUR FREE BOOKS!

2 FREE NOVELS PLUS 2 FREE GIFTS!

Sparked by Danger, Fueled by Passion.

YES! Please send me 2 FREE Silhouette® Romantic Suspense novels and my 2 FREE gifts (gifts are worth about $10). After receiving them, if I don't wish to receive any more books, I can return the shipping statement marked "cancel." If I don't cancel, I will receive 4 brand-new novels every month and be billed just $4.24 per book in the U.S. or $4.99 per book in Canada. That's a saving of 15% off the cover price! It's quite a bargain! Shipping and handling is just 50¢ per book.* I understand that accepting the 2 free books and gifts places me under no obligation to buy anything. I can always return a shipment and cancel at any time. Even if I never buy another book from Silhouette, the two free books and gifts are mine to keep forever.

240/340 SDN E5Q4

Name _____ (PLEASE PRINT) _____

Address _____ Apt. #

City _____ State/Prov. _____ Zip/Postal Code

Signature (if under 18, a parent or guardian must sign)

Mail to the **Silhouette Reader Service:**
IN U.S.A.: P.O. Box 1867, Buffalo, NY 14240-1867
IN CANADA: P.O. Box 609, Fort Erie, Ontario L2A 5X3

Not valid for current subscribers to Silhouette Romantic Suspense books.

Want to try two free books from another line?
Call 1-800-873-8635 or visit www.morefreebooks.com.

* Terms and prices subject to change without notice. Prices do not include applicable taxes. N.Y. residents add applicable sales tax. Canadian residents will be charged applicable provincial taxes and GST. Offer not valid in Quebec. This offer is limited to one order per household. All orders subject to approval. Credit or debit balances in a customer's account(s) may be offset by any other outstanding balance owed by or to the customer. Please allow 4 to 6 weeks for delivery. Offer available while quantities last.

Your Privacy: Silhouette is committed to protecting your privacy. Our Privacy Policy is available online at www.eHarlequin.com or upon request from the Reader Service. From time to time we make our lists of customers available to reputable third parties who may have a product or service of interest to you. If you would prefer we not share your name and address, please check here. ☐

Help us get it right—We strive for accurate, respectful and relevant communications. To clarify or modify your communication preferences, visit us at www.ReaderService.com/consumerchoice.

SRS10R

*Harlequin Romance author Donna Alward is loved
for her gorgeous rancher heroes.*

*Meet Wyatt as he's confronted by both a precious
little pink bundle left on his doorstep and his neighbor Elli
who's going to show him the ropes....*

Introducing
PROUD RANCHER, PRECIOUS BUNDLE

THE SQUAWKING QUIETED as Elli picked the baby up, and
Wyatt turned around, trying hard to ignore the feelings of
inadequacy as Darcy immediately stopped fussing.

"Maybe she's uncomfortable. What do you think, sweetheart?" Elli turned her conversation to the baby.

"What do you think is wrong?" Wyatt asked, putting the
coffee pot back on the burner.

A strange look passed over Elli's face, one that looked
like guilt and panic. But it was gone quickly. "I couldn't
say," she replied.

"But you were so good with her this afternoon." Wyatt
put his hands on his hips.

"Lucky, that's all. I just…remembered a few things."
The same strange look flitted over her features once more.

Wyatt took the coffee to the table. "You fooled me. You
looked like you knew exactly what you were doing." So
much so that Wyatt had felt completely inept. A feeling he
despised. He was used to being the one in control.

Elli and Darcy walked the length of the kitchen and
back. After a few moments, she admitted, "I haven't really
cared for a baby before. The things I thought of were simply
things I'd heard about. Not from experience, Mr. Black."

Her chin jutted up, closing the subject but making him

want to ask the questions now pulsing through his mind. But then he remembered the old saying—*Don't look a gift horse in the mouth.* He'd benefit from whatever insight she had and be glad of it.

"I don't really know what babies need," he said. "I fed her, patted her back like you did, walked her to sleep, but every time I put her down…"

Wyatt almost groaned. Of course. He'd forgotten one important thing. He'd been so focused on getting the formula the right temperature that he'd forgotten to check her diaper. Not that he had any clue what to do there either.

Pulling calves and shoveling out stalls was far less intimidating than one tiny newborn.

"She's probably due for a diaper change, isn't she." He tried to sound nonchalant. This was a perfect opportunity. Elli must know how to change a diaper. He could simply watch her so he'd know better for the next time.

Instead, Elli came around the corner of the counter and placed Darcy back in his arms. "Here you go, Uncle Wyatt," she said lightly. "You get diaper duty. I'll fix the coffee. Cream and sugar?"

Oh boy, Wyatt thought, looking down into Darcy's pursed face, his smug plan blown to smithereens. He was in for it now.

Will sparks fly between Elli and Wyatt?

Find out in
PROUD RANCHER, PRECIOUS BUNDLE
Available February 2011 from Harlequin Romance

Copyright © 2011 by Donna Alward

HREXP0211

Try these Healthy and Delicious Spring Rolls!

INGREDIENTS

2 packages rice-paper spring roll wrappers (20 wrappers)

1 cup grated carrot

¼ cup bean sprouts

1 cucumber, julienned

1 red bell pepper, without stem and seeds, julienned

4 green onions finely chopped— use only the green part

DIRECTIONS

1. Soak one rice-paper wrapper in a large bowl of hot water until softened.

2. Place a pinch each of carrots, sprouts, cucumber, bell pepper and green onion on the wrapper toward the bottom third of the rice paper.

3. Fold ends in and roll tightly to enclose filling.

4. Repeat with remaining wrappers. Chill before serving.

Find this and many more delectable recipes including the perfect dipping sauce in

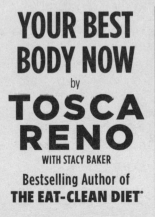

YOUR BEST BODY NOW
by
TOSCA RENO

WITH STACY BAKER

**Bestselling Author of
THE EAT-CLEAN DIET®**

Available wherever books are sold!

NTRSERIESJAN

SPECIAL EDITION

FROM *USA TODAY* BESTSELLING AUTHOR
CHRISTINE RIMMER
COMES AN ALL-NEW BRAVO FAMILY TIES STORY.

Donovan McRae has experienced
the greatest loss a man can face, and
while he can't forgive himself, life—
and Abilene Bravo's love—are still
waiting for him. Can he find it in himself
to reach out and claim them?

Look for
DONOVAN'S CHILD
available February 2011

Visit Silhouette Books at www.eHarlequin.com

SSE65577

Silhouette® ROMANTIC SUSPENSE

Sparked by Danger, Fueled by Passion.

NEW YORK TIMES BESTSELLING AUTHOR

RACHEL LEE
No Ordinary Hero

Strange noises…a woman's mysterious disappearance and a killer on the loose who's too close for comfort.

With no where else to turn, Delia Carmody looks to her aloof neighbour to help, only to discover that Mike Windwalker is no ordinary hero.

Conard County *THE NEXT GENERATION*

Available in February.
Wherever books are sold.

Visit Silhouette Books at www.eHarlequin.com

SRS27709R2

USA TODAY bestselling author

Sharon Kendrick

introduces

HIS MAJESTY'S CHILD

The king's baby of shame!

King Casimiro harbors a secret—no one in the kingdom
of Zaffirinthos knows that a devastating accident has left
his memory clouded in darkness. And Casimiro himself
cannot answer why Melissa Maguire, an enigmatic English
rose, stirs such feelings in him…. Questioning his ability
to rule, Casimiro decides he will renounce the throne.
But Melissa has news she knows will rock the palace
to its core—*Casimiro has an heir!*

Law dictates Casimiro cannot abdicate, so he must find a
way to reacquaint himself with Melissa—his new queen!

Available from Harlequin Presents
February 2011

www.eHarlequin.com

HP12972